NANTUCKET WHITE CHRISTMAS

PAMELA M. KELLEY

PIPING PLOVER PRESS

Born on Christmas, Angela Stark has always hated the holiday. Bad things always seem to happen and this year is no exception when she is fired and evicted on the first day of December.

She was living and working as a maid in San Francisco. Who will hire her at this time of year, especially if they learn why she was fired?

Her only family is Sam, an elderly, and quite vocal orange cat. Her only option is to stay temporarily with her best friend Jane, but she is extremely allergic to cats. It's not ideal, but it doesn't look like she has a choice, until a certified letter arrives that changes everything.

The next thing she knows, she and Sam are flying to Nantucket, a place they've never been before.

It's meant to be a temporary visit. But then Angela meets the Hodges family and friends and begins to question where home really is.

1

---

randma got run over by a reindeer…"

The cheerful Christmas carol blasted through the ancient speakers of Angela Stark's tired old Saturn sedan. She changed the channel as quickly as possible. It was annoying that her favorite station started playing nothing but Christmas music as soon as Thanksgiving rolled around. She'd already suffered through a week of it and it was only December first.

Angela felt positively Scrooge-like as she sat in the San Francisco morning rush hour traffic. She hated this time of year. It was bad enough that her birthday fell on Christmas itself. Growing up as an orphan and bouncing from one foster home to the next, her birthday usually got lost in the shuffle. Nothing good ever seemed to happen around the holidays. For as long as she could recall, her memories of the time of year were not happy ones, beginning with her mother over-dosing on Christmas Eve when Angela was barely five years old.

It had just been the two of them, and Chrissy had never been the motherly type. She was sweet enough, child-like almost when she was sober, but that wasn't often. Chrissy was a junkie, addicted to heroin and even as a child, Angela knew that wasn't a good thing. She still remembered the day that she found her mother, and the vivid image of her seemingly asleep on the sofa, holding a half-eaten candy-cane. Angela had tried her best to wake her, but Chrissy was gone.

And since there was no other known family, little Angela went into foster care. As soon as she was eighteen, she moved into an apartment with several friends. She was working by then, hostessing at a local restaurant. There was no money for college, but she'd done well enough in school to get a small scholarship which helped to pay for some classes at the local community college. Eventually, though, she'd had to drop to part-time and started working full-time as a maid for a cleaning company.

Now, at age twenty-eight, she only had two classes left for her Bachelor's Degree in Business. Once she graduated, she planned to get a job in marketing at one of the many software companies in Silicon Valley. She'd tried a few times to get something entry-level over the years, but every company seemed to want a college degree.

So, for now, cleaning other people's houses paid the bills, or at least it had until her roommate skipped out on her. Because of Susie's disappearing act, Angela was almost three months behind on half the rent. But she had someone lined up to move in tomorrow and her first and last month's deposit should catch her up. Angela knew she was supposed to set it aside in a separate account, but she figured she could do that in a few months and all would be well. Of the people that answered her ad, Kim was the person who seemed the most stable and could move in the quickest. Robert Smith, the building's property manager, had been calling daily looking for money that Angela didn't have. But she would have it soon enough, hopefully.

And truth be told, Angela didn't mind cleaning. She was good at it, and she found it relaxing and satisfying to leave a home spotless. She had a busy day ahead of her, with several large homes she cleaned regularly. The first on her list was for one of her least favorite clients. The house was gorgeous, but the owner was annoying and her teenage daughter was an absolute slob. Usually, they weren't there when Angela cleaned but today mother and daughter were both home when Angela arrived and the mother was screaming upstairs to her daughter to hurry up.

"We have mani-pedi appointments and if she doesn't get down here we're going to be late," Mrs. Davis explained. "Julia, now!"

Two minutes later, a sullen, skinny, sixteen-year-old

with long purple streaks in her dark brown hair came trudging down the stairs with a backpack slung over one shoulder. She glanced at Angela and several emotions flashed across her face—surprise, followed by what looked like guilt, which quickly morphed into annoyance as her mother told her to hurry again.

"I'll take my own car," Julia said. "I'm going to meet up with Stacy later."

"Now you tell me. I could have already left." Mrs. Davis sighed and turned back to Angela. "Be sure to scrub the bathtub in the guest bathroom. We have company coming."

"Will do." Angela felt like adding that she always scrubbed it, but bit her tongue. She just wanted them to leave so she could blast her music and focus on cleaning.

When she was finished with her last house, at a little past four, Angela walked into the cleaning company headquarters to drop off her keys. She picked them up for each home in the morning and returned them at the end of the day. She'd worked for Happy Cleaners for over four years and was one of their longest tenured employees.

The owner of the company, Nora Feeney, was a skinny, chain-smoking bundle of nerves. Everything seemed to agitate her, but Angela was used to it and just smiled when she walked into the office. No one smiled back today, though. Instead, Nora, her husband Tom, and the receptionist, Mary, all looked uncomfortable when they saw Angela. There was a definite chill in the air.

With a sense of foreboding, Angela walked over to the wall where the keys were hung and put her three in their spots. When she turned around, Mary was staring at her computer and Tom had left the room. Nora hadn't moved and was standing with her bony arms crossed over her chest.

"Angela, could you step into my office for a moment, please?"

"Of course." Angela followed her boss into her office and stood, waiting for Nora to speak.

"This is a bit awkward," Nora began. "I've never actually had this situation happen before and it's unfortunate as you've been a good, consistent cleaner for us. But, we don't really have a choice, I'm afraid."

Angela had no idea what Nora was talking about, but shivered as a chill ran down her spine. She said nothing, and waited for Nora to explain.

"I had a call from Mrs. Davis. You cleaned her place this morning?"

Angela nodded. "I did. They were first on my list. I saw her and her daughter briefly, before they headed out."

"Yes, well, Mrs. Davis called this afternoon and she wasn't happy with us at all. Or more specifically, with you."

Angela narrowed her eyes, feeling irritated at the annoying woman. What was it this time? She'd scrubbed that guest bathtub until it gleamed. "What was she upset about?"

"She said her diamond tennis bracelet is missing. It was on her nightstand when she left and when she got home, it was gone. The only other person in the house was you. They have an alarm system and cameras that noted everyone who came and went and it was only you."

Angela's jaw dropped. "Are you saying she's accusing me of taking her bracelet? I didn't touch it and I never even saw it on her nightstand." She thought for a moment and it didn't take her long to figure out where the bracelet went. The guilty look on Julia Davis's face as she came down the stairs—either Mrs. Davis was mistaken about where she put her bracelet or her daughter lifted it before she walked out.

"She can't prove anything of course, but she is insisting that we fire you. She said if we don't, she'll stop using us and will tell everyone she has referred to stop using us, too." Nora looked miserable as she said it and Angela almost felt sorry for her. Almost.

"She's furious and we simply can't afford to lose that much business. I'm so sorry, Angela. If anything changes, and we're able to rehire you, I'll be in touch. I really do hope that is the case."

Angela nodded. "I understand. When you tell her that you've let me go, you might want to also tell her to ask her daughter Julia if she's seen the bracelet."

"I will, and again, Angela, I'm so sorry."

∾

Angela drove home in a daze and didn't realize until she pulled up to her condo and grabbed her phone and purse that she had a new text message. It was from Kim, the roommate who was supposed to move in the next day.

"Angela, I'm so sorry to do this last minute, but I'm not going to be able to move in with you after all. My boyfriend proposed last night and asked me to move in with him instead. I hope you understand and again, I'm so sorry. Could you please just rip up the check I gave you? Thank you!"

Angela laughed before she almost started to cry. Could her day possibly get any worse?

As it turned out, it could.

She wasn't home ten minutes before there was a knock on the door and her heart sank as she opened it. She didn't have to guess who it was. Only one person would be knocking on her door. Sure enough, Robert Smith, the property manager, stood there with his thinning hair and permanent scowl.

"Hi, Angela. I hope you've got something for me today? It's the last day for you to bring your account current."

Angela took a deep breath and willed the tears to stay down. Crying wasn't going to help.

"I thought that I'd have a check for you today, but my new roommate changed her mind. So, I have to turn the ad on again. I need a little more time, please."

Robert Smith actually looked disappointed as he shook his head and reached into the rumpled manila folder that was tucked under his arm. He pulled out a typed letter and handed it to her.

"What's this?" Angela asked as she glanced at the letter. The words grew blurry as the first tears fell.

"I'm sorry, Angela. I gave you all the time that I could. That's your official eviction notice. You have two weeks to pack up and get out."

Angela just nodded. She'd had several extensions already and he had warned that eviction would be the next step. But she'd thought she would be able to avoid it with the new roommate moving in.

"I understand."

"Good luck, Angela." He walked off as Angela closed the door behind her. Her day had gone from bad to horrific and she had no idea what to do next.

2

At least you still love me." Angela scooped up Sam, her twelve-year-old orange cat who'd been rubbing against her legs and meowing since she walked in the door. When she held him close to her, he butted his head against her chin until she scratched it the way he liked. He allowed her to hold him for another minute before he wiggled to get down and ran over to his food bowl. Once he was fed and full, he joined her on the sofa where she had collapsed and was gloomily scrolling through the help-wanted job listings on her laptop.

Angela was starting to get scared. She only had one week until she had to move out and she wasn't having any luck even getting an interview, let alone a job offer. She'd known it would be hard, but thought she'd get at least one call. She even visited a few temporary agencies and said she'd be willing to take anything they had.

But since she'd just been cleaning houses for the past few years, she didn't have any office experience and that's what most of their clients looked for. They all promised to call if anything came in, but in the next breath warned her not to get her hopes up as it was also the slowest time of the year.

She applied for unemployment, but that wouldn't kick in for another few weeks. Her best friend, Jane, insisted that she come to stay with her until she could get back on her feet and save enough to get a new place. Angela and Sam had lived with Jane for several years, before she moved in with her boyfriend and realized she had a terrible allergy to cats. All her symptoms disappeared once she'd moved out so Angela felt guilty now about bringing Sam, but there was no way she was going anywhere without him. Sam was her only family. She was grateful for Jane's offer, though, and reluctantly accepted as she had no other choice.

"It will be fun! And we have plenty of room, with a guest bedroom that never gets used. It will be almost like old times." Jane seemed genuinely enthusiastic about the idea.

"I'll pay for the allergy meds!" Angela insisted.

"Don't be silly. I take them anyway. I'm allergic to more than cats. And I like Sam."

So, it was decided. To raise money, Angela had a huge moving sale over the weekend and sold everything that she could, including her bed, TV and sofa, though she'd arranged for those items to be picked up on her move out day. When she found a new place, she'd really be starting over, but she had no other choice. She couldn't afford to move everything and pay to have it stored. She'd have to look for a furnished situation, maybe a room in an existing apartment, something pet-friendly.

Three days before she was due to move in with Jane, Angela was sprawled on the sofa again with Sam behind her, peering down at her laptop while she applied for job after job. A knock on the door surprised and irritated her. She was comfy and didn't want to get up, and she figured it was someone knocking on the wrong door because she wasn't expecting anyone.

A peek through the window showed it was Al, the mailman. She opened the door and he held out a certified envelope.

"Hi, Angela. I need your signature here."

"What is that?" She'd never received anything by certified mail before.

"No idea, honey. I just deliver it."

She scribbled her signature and glanced at the return address. It was a law firm on Beacon Street, in Boston. She didn't know anyone in Boston and had never even been to the East Coast.

"Thanks, Al." She closed the door and brought the letter over to the sofa where Sam was busy stretching and looking cute. She sat and slowly opened the envelope. She had the sense that it was something important or it wouldn't have come by certified mail, but she couldn't imagine what it could be. She slid out a thick, creamy sheet of letterhead, unfolded it and read the letter three times and then once again, because it still didn't make sense.

> *Dear Angela,*
>
> *I am writing to inform you that your grandmother, Estelle Stark, has recently died and you are the sole beneficiary for her estate which includes her residence on Nantucket, her vehicle, and a local bank account. Should you wish to sell the home, Estelle had mentioned that it does need some repairs. There should be enough in the account to cover those repairs and other living expenses for several months. Please call me at your earliest convenience so I can arrange to send you the keys to the home and give you the banking details.*
>
> *Very truly yours,*
> *Warren Higgins, Esq.*

WHEN ANGELA WAS able to stop shaking long enough to punch in the phone number for the Boston law office, she called Warren Higgins and waited, feeling sure that there must have been some mistake. How could she have inherited a house from a woman she never knew? And if she really had a grandmother, why hadn't she reached out to her while she was alive? Especially after Chrissy died, when she really needed her?

Warren was in a meeting, but his receptionist

promised to have him call back as soon as he was free. Angela didn't expect that she'd hear from him for a while, but ten minutes later her phone rang and it was him.

"I'm sure there must be a mistake," she began when Warren introduced himself.

"I can assure you that there is no mistake. Your mother was Chrissy, right?" he asked kindly.

"Yes, but why am I just hearing about her now? Why did my grandmother never contact me before?"

Warren sighed. "She never knew about you until just before she died and it broke her heart. She found out accidentally, through one of those ancestry kits. Her best friend told her to check the box to see if she had any living relatives. It was a bet of sorts, because she was certain that she did not."

"A DNA kit? Jane and I did one of those a few years ago." Angela remembered that Jane had talked her into it and it was through an online Cyber Monday sale. "I was mostly curious to see if I really was part Irish. My mother used to say that I was black Irish, because of my dark hair, light skin and green eyes."

"It sounds like you took after your grandmother. She was born in Ireland."

"So, this grandmother I never knew, remembered me in her will? And really left me a house?"

"It's true. It's a lovely cottage from what I've seen of the pictures online. Your grandmother was quite proud of her roses."

"She grew roses." Angela tried to picture it in her mind, a tiny cottage with a rose bush or two.

"Will you be going to Nantucket soon to see the house? I'm assuming since you live on the West Coast that you might be looking to put it on the market?"

Angela laughed. "I can't really afford to make the trip right now. I'll probably put it on the market immediately, though. I need the money," she admitted.

"Oh, well, then. You should be there to oversee the repairs. I could transfer some of the funds to your account, so that you can buy a one-way ticket for now. And I'll overnight the keys to you."

"I suppose I should do that. Thank you." Angela's head was spinning. She'd been mentally preparing herself to move into Jane's guest room and now she and Sam needed to fly clear across the country. It was a lot to take in. She gave Warren the information he needed and when she hung up, she walked in a daze back to her sofa.

She Googled the Nantucket address of her grandmother's cottage and her jaw dropped. It was considerably more substantial than what she'd pictured as a small cottage. It had three bedrooms, with two of them on a second floor. It was a short walk to the beach and had pretty harbor views. The yard was large and her grandmother's roses were beautiful, spilling out of flower boxes and along a pretty, white picket fence. It was lovely. And the estimated worth for the property was staggering, almost two million dollars.

Nantucket was apparently more expensive than San Francisco. Angela smiled and felt like she'd won the lottery. If she made the repairs and sold the cottage, she could return to San Francisco and her financial worries would be gone. She could easily pay the market rent for whatever she wanted or maybe even buy a small place, and she could focus on finishing school without stressing about how she was going to afford it all. It was truly a blessing.

3

Angela woke up the next day and wondered if she'd dreamed about the letter and her grandmother's cottage. It seemed too surreal to be true. But when the keys arrived the next day via Fed-Ex and money appeared in her banking account in the amount Warren mentioned, it finally sunk in that it was all very real.

She got busy getting ready, ordering airline tickets for her and for Sam and contacting his veterinarian to get a letter stating that Sam was fit to fly. Jane was going to use Angela's car while she was gone, as hers died a few weeks back. Angela happily offered the use of hers as she was just going to leave it at Jane's anyway.

Jane drove Angela and Sam to the airport. She just had one big suitcase and Sam's soft cat carrier. She was glad that she was able to bring him on the plane with her and keep him in her lap. She hated the thought of him scared somewhere in the cargo section.

When they reached the JetBlue terminal, Jane pulled up to the curb and helped Angela get her luggage and Sam's carrier from the car. Jane had damp eyes as she pulled Angela in for a goodbye hug.

"I can't believe this is happening to you. It's amazing and I'm thrilled for you. I just hope you don't fall in love with Nantucket and decide to stay there. I'm already missing you!"

Angela laughed. "I'll be back as soon as possible. Once I sell the cottage, I'll finally be able to afford to live here."

"Have a safe trip and send lots of pictures!"

～

THE VET HAD ALSO GIVEN Angela medicine that would calm Sam and make him drowsy so he could sleep through most of the flight. Once they were settled in their seat, she reached in and rubbed a little of the calming gel on his ear and spoke softly to him. He didn't particularly care for the takeoff but once they were up in the air, he drifted off to sleep and Angela was glad to have him on her lap. She was a nervous flier and it was comforting to have him there.

The flight was a long one, almost six hours, and when they landed in Boston it was late afternoon. Unlike most cities that were planned grids, Boston's streets looked like a giant tangle from the sky and the air was so much cooler. She shivered as a blast of cold air blew through the thin material of the walkway as she stepped off the plane.

There was no direct flight to Nantucket, so she was going to catch a small shuttle flight on Cape Air. Sam woke as they were walking to their connecting flight and immediately protested by meowing loudly. She stopped to reapply some calming gel and he drifted off again a few minutes later.

Thirty minutes later, she was settled onto the shuttle flight and an older woman who looked to be in her early fifties or so sat next to her. The plane was very small, with only about nine seats. Angela knew that the flight would be about forty-five minutes and half the time would be taxiing down the runway, and taking off and landing.

"Are you visiting friends on Nantucket?" the woman asked pleasantly. She had a nice smile and kind eyes.

"No. I don't know anyone there, actually. My grandmother used to live there, Estelle Stark. She passed away recently."

"I'm so sorry for your loss. I knew Estelle well. She was a neighbor and a lovely lady. I'm Lisa Hodges. I live right down the road from your grandmother."

"Angela Stark. I know this may sound strange, but I didn't actually know my grandmother. I only just found out that she existed when her lawyer contacted me and left me her house. Her lawyer said she didn't know about me, either, until just before she died."

Angela could see sympathy reflected in Lisa's eyes.

"She never mentioned having a granddaughter. I'm sure if she did know, she would have contacted you sooner. I am sorry that you didn't get to know her."

"Thanks. It has come as a bit of a shock. Do you have any children?"

"I do. Four of them. My twins, Kate and Kristen, are the oldest, in their mid-thirties. Chase is two years younger and Abby is the baby. She just recently turned thirty. She's the only one so far that's married and she just had Natalie, my first grandchild, on Thanksgiving."

"How exciting! Do you all live on Nantucket?"

Lisa nodded. "We do. Kate only just moved home this past year. She was working in Boston at a fashion magazine and loved it, until they were sold and had layoffs. Now she does some freelancing and writes mystery novels."

"She does? I love mysteries. I wonder if I've read any of them?"

"She only has one out so far, Hidden Memories, but she's working on another."

"It sounds familiar, but I haven't read that one."

"My daughter, Kristen, is an artist, and she's lucky that she's able to do it full time now. Her boyfriend, Tyler Everly, is also a writer. Maybe you've heard of him?"

Angela laughed. "Of course! Everyone knows him. I love his books. I didn't know he lived on Nantucket."

"He hasn't been here all that long, maybe six months. He bought the cottage next to Kristen and that's how they met. She dated his brother first. He owns an art gallery downtown. They only went on one date, I think. It was never anything serious," Lisa quickly explained.

"What does your son, Chase, do?" Angela asked.

"He's a builder. Runs his own small business and he's very good at what he does," she said proudly.

Angela smiled. It was clear that Lisa adored her children. "He actually just mentioned recently after a storm that it looked like your grandmother's roof lost some shingles."

"Her lawyer said that it might need some repairs and that I would probably want to do that before I sold it."

"Are you planning to sell?"

"Yes. To be perfectly honest, I need the money. As soon as I sell, I'll be heading back to San Francisco, getting a new place and finishing school. I only have a few classes left."

"Oh? What are you studying?"

"Business, with a marketing concentration. I hope to get a marketing job at one of the Silicon Valley tech companies."

"That sounds like a good plan. I should give you Chase's number in case you want to call him for an estimate on those repairs. You'll talk to his office manager, Beth, and she'll get you onto his calendar. She's wonderful and we're crossing our fingers that they'll be the next to announce their engagement."

"Oh, thank you. Did one of your other children just get engaged?" Angela wasn't sure what Lisa meant by 'next'.

Lisa laughed. "No. It was actually me, just a few weeks ago, on Thanksgiving. I turned my house into a bed and breakfast and my first guest was a gentleman named Rhett that was opening a restaurant on Nantucket, so he stayed for the summer. We struck up a friendship, and—well, at my age, it doesn't take long before you know it's right."

"Congratulations!" Angela was enjoying talking to Lisa, and was surprised to see after they chatted a while longer that the flight was almost over. The plane was beginning its descent to Nantucket.

"How were you planning to get home, dear?"

"I figured I'd just call a cab at the airport."

"Rhett is picking me up, and we'd be happy to drop you off."

"Thank you, but I don't want to be a bother."

Lisa laughed. "It's not a bother at all. We are going right by." She pulled out a piece of paper and jotted down a few phone numbers.

"Here's my son Chase's number, and also his ex-girlfriend, Lauren Snyder. I'm not sorry they broke up, as Beth is a much better match for him. But Lauren is a hustler and if you need your house sold fast, she is probably the best person to get it done. And here's my number, too, in case you need it. Do you have plans on Saturday?"

Angela smiled. "I have no plans at all."

"Why don't you come by for breakfast around nine? My girls will be there then. They usually stop by on Saturdays and they're about your age. It will be nice for you to meet some people here if you're going to be around for a few months."

"I'd love that."

~

WHEN THEY GOT off the plane and found their luggage, they went outside. Lisa's face lit up when she saw a handsome older man waving at them. They made their way over to him and Lisa introduced them.

"Rhett, this is Angela Stark, Estelle Stark's granddaughter. She's going to be staying at Estelle's house for a bit. I told her we'd be glad to drop her off on our way home."

"Nice to meet you. Your grandmother was a nice lady. She took good care of those knockout roses." He looked at Lisa. "We should think about putting some of those by the fence."

"That's a great idea, if you don't mind taking care of it. I have a black thumb."

He laughed. "I'm not sure what color mine is, but we can give it a try."

Rhett put their bags in his car and Angela sat in the back seat with Sam. He was starting to stir a little. She reached in and gave him a pat and he settled right down again. Less than ten minutes later, Rhett pulled up in front of her grandmother's cottage. It was getting dark so she couldn't get a good look at it. All the roses were, of course, gone due to the time of year, but the house looked bigger than it had appeared online and had a welcoming feel to it.

Rhett insisted on carrying her bag to the front steps and Lisa gave her a hug before they left.

"If you need anything, you have our number. See you on Saturday."

They waited until she had the door unlocked before they drove away. Angela took a deep breath. It was hard to believe she actually owned a real house. She flipped on the lights and smiled as she stepped inside with Sam in his carrier. She set him down and wheeled her suitcase in, then took a good look around. The house was lovely inside.

There were well worn hard wood floors and soft throw rugs, an oversized, cream-colored sofa and a glass-and-wood coffee table. The kitchen was roomy and light with all white cabinets and pale blue trim. She let Sam out of his carrier, and he woke up and followed her around the rest of the house, running into every nook and cranny, sniffing everywhere.

Angela went upstairs and found two good-sized bedrooms with lovely, distant water views and a shared bathroom. There was a master bedroom downstairs with an attached bath and huge bay windows. There was also a mudroom off the kitchen and an office beyond that. She decided to set up Sam's litter box in the mudroom, and got the box and a small bag of litter from her suitcase.

She was planning to go exploring the next day and knew there was a grocery store where she could stock up on everything that she needed. She also knew her grandmother had left a car, a blue Mini Cooper. She had a feeling that it was probably going to need to be jumped to get it started after sitting idle for several months, but she could call someone in the morning to do that.

Suddenly the day caught up to her and she felt exhausted. There was boxes of pasta and jars of sauce in her grandmother's kitchen, but Angela didn't have the energy to cook anything. She still had a banana and a granola bar in her tote bag and ate those for dinner. She stripped her grandmother's bed and threw the sheets in the wash while she ate, and a little while later put the laundry in the dryer while she unpacked her suitcase and watched a little TV. When the sheets were dry, she made her bed and flopped into it. Sam hopped up on the pillow next to her and a few minutes later, they were both fast asleep.

4

So, do you want to go to that food and wine event Sunday night? I need to let my cousin know today if we want the tickets. Philippe, do you want to go?" Jessica's irritation was evident.

"Sorry, do I want to go where?" Philippe looked up from his laptop and met Jessica's icy blue glare. How could someone so beautiful look so cold? Her blonde hair fell in perfect curls to her shoulders and her pale blue sweater, cashmere probably, hugged her slim curves. And she was wearing high heels, of course. They looked painful to him, but they did magical things to her very toned legs.

"To the Taste of the Town! On Sunday. I've mentioned it to you several times."

"Sure, that sounds good." He turned his attention back to his laptop.

"What are you looking at that's so interesting?" Jessica still sounded annoyed. It was early. She'd spent the night and was heading off to work, while he didn't have to go anywhere except across the kitchen for more coffee. He turned his laptop around to show her the screen.

"What do you think? Should I go with Ralph with the short hair or Mandy with the long?"

The expression on Jessica's face was priceless. "Cats? That's what had your attention? You're not seriously thinking of getting one?"

"I am. It's been a few months since I lost Oscar and I'm thinking I'm ready." The local shelter had pictures of the animals that were available for adoption and Philippe really wanted to bring one home soon.

Jessica's nose wrinkled as if she'd smelled something particularly foul. "I don't understand why anyone would want a cat. They're demanding and selfish, and their litter boxes stink!"

"Well, Oscar was an outdoor cat. It's safe on Nantucket as we don't have coyotes here."

"Hm. Well, don't you travel too much to get another cat? Are you going to be here longer now?" She perked up at the thought, which set off a distant alarm bell. It also reminded him that she was right, sort of.

"I'm not sure yet on that. I might be sticking around longer. So, I guess I should hold off at least until I know for sure."

"Well, I should probably head out." Jessica took a step back and almost tripped over one of his sweatshirts that had fallen on the floor. She grabbed hold of the kitchen island to steady herself and shook her head at him.

"You really should call someone to come and clean for you. Judy's only been gone a week and this place is a pigsty!"

Philippe glanced around the room. Once again, Jessica had a valid point. His housekeeper, Judy, was in Florida for six weeks visiting her family over the holidays. And in the week she'd been gone, his pack rat tendencies had taken over. There were jackets and sweatshirts strewn around the room, boxes and mail piled up on the kitchen table and a bag of trash by the door that he needed to take out. When he was deep into the writing of a book, clutter happened.

"I'll think about that. It's a good idea."

Jessica smiled and wrapped her arms around him. "Good. I'm off, then. Thanks again for dinner last night. That wine was amazing."

"You're very welcome. That Belle Glos was pretty good, huh?"

"Delicious! See you on Sunday." She gave him a goodbye kiss and he watched her leave, then turned his attention back to his computer, switching from the cat profiles to his manuscript. He wasn't quite ready to dive in yet, though, so he pulled up Facebook and smiled when he saw a message from Kate Hodges. He'd mentored her a bit as she wrote her first mystery novel and he'd enjoyed their conversations.

He'd first met Kate when she was doing an interview on the Nantucket Film Festival, which he was involved with. He'd asked her on a date after the interview because she was attractive and smart, but Kate soon let him know that she just wanted to be friends. As always, he was honest with the women he dated that he wasn't looking for anything serious and that didn't work for Kate. It was too soon after a breakup for her, as well. She started dating Jack Trattel not too long after and now they were living together. He was happy for both of them. Jack was a good guy and one of his regular poker buddies. He clicked open her message.

"Hey, Philippe, just wondering if you're around and maybe available for lunch? I'm stuck at the moment and would love to brainstorm with you a bit."

He immediately wrote back. "Would love to. How about meeting at The Brotherhood of Thieves at noon? I haven't had one of their burgers in a while."

"Perfect. See you then."

∼

WHEN HE ARRIVED at the restaurant, Kate was already seated in a booth. He gave her a quick hug hello and apologized for running a few minutes late.

"I hope you weren't waiting too long," he said as he sat across from her.

"No, not at all. I got here maybe two minutes before you."

When their server came, they both put in their orders without even needing to look at the menu. Philippe got his usual cheeseburger and Kate got one of their special burgers with Boursin cheese, caramelized onions and sautéed mushrooms. While they waited for their food to come, Kate filled him in on where she was stuck in her story and he made a few suggestions. They were just finishing up when their food arrived.

"Thank you. It always helps to talk things out. How is your book coming along?" Kate asked.

"Not too bad. You saved me from a morning of putting it off. When I saw your message I decided to buckle down and get a few hours in before meeting you for lunch."

Kate laughed. "I do the same thing. It's worse when I'm not sure where I'm going though, like today."

Philippe nodded. He didn't really know why he always had a hard time getting started each day. He was fine once he typed his first sentence.

"I think it's like going to the gym. It's hard to make yourself go, but you're always glad you went." He bit into his burger. It was excellent as usual.

"That's so true. Are you still seeing Jessica Lavin? Kristen thought she saw the two of you walking down Main Street last night.

He nodded. "We had dinner last night. Went to Keeper's. Good, as usual."

Kate cocked her head and looked at him curiously. "Are things getting serious with her?"

"No more than with anyone else. She's a beautiful girl and we're enjoying each other's company. She knows I don't want anything serious."

"Hm. I wonder sometimes if that makes you even more attractive to some girls. More of a challenge. They think they can change you."

"I hope not." Philippe thought about Jessica's enthusiasm when he said he might be around longer. He knew she liked being seen with him. He was often recognized when they went out and they both liked going to good restaurants. He might need to cool things down, though, if he sensed she was looking for more than he was willing to give. He remembered what she said about getting a cleaner, though.

"Any chance you know of someone who could fill in for Judy by cleaning twice a week until she gets back? Jessica pointed out that my place is a disaster. And she's quite right about that."

Kate laughed. "I don't know of anyone off-hand, but I'm seeing my mother and sisters tomorrow for breakfast. I can ask if they know of anyone."

"Thanks. I'd appreciate that."

"No problem." Kate set her burger down and smiled. "I can't wait for you to meet someone that will really knock you off your feet. You'll want to settle down then."

"I'd love for that to happen, but I just don't see it happening."

5

Angela woke to soft sunlight streaming in through the oversized windows in her grandmother's bedroom. She stretched lazily and saw that Sam was still sound asleep on the pillow beside her. She yawned, slowly eased out of bed and padded to the kitchen. She'd slept really well, which surprised her as she hadn't been sleeping well lately. But she supposed maybe the clean, crisp Nantucket air and realization that her financial problems were finally over might have helped.

She looked around the kitchen for coffee and was impressed when she found a box of K-cups and a newer model Keurig machine. Her grandmother clearly had appreciated a good cup of coffee. She fed Sam while it was brewing, then brought her cup over to the kitchen table and fired up her laptop. First thing on her list was to call someone to come give her grandmother's car a jump.

She'd checked it the night before and, as expected, it was dead as could be. It was a cute car, though—a blue-gray Mini Cooper convertible. The auto repair place said they'd send someone within thirty minutes. She pulled out the sheet of paper from Lisa with the phone numbers and called her son, Chase, next. His office manager, Beth, answered and Angela told her that Lisa had suggested she call and why.

"Hold on, let me check Chase's schedule. It looks like he'll be in your area mid-morning. I could have him swing by around eleven, if that works?"

"That would be great, thanks." Angela hung up and called Lauren next. She seemed thrilled and a bit surprised to hear that Lisa had referred her.

"Well, isn't that a nice surprise. Of course I'd love to help. I could stop by today around eleven thirty or twelve?"

"Eleven thirty sounds good." She gave Lauren the address, then realized as soon as she hung up that Chase was coming at eleven. Hopefully that wouldn't be a problem.

Fortunately, her grandmother's car was fine, other than a dead battery. It roared to life once it was charged up and Angela kept it running for a half hour or so to fully charge the battery.

At eleven sharp, she heard a car pull into the driveway and saw from the window that it was a truck with Hodges Builders printed along the side. A tall man with blond hair and a navy sweatshirt with the same company name on it walked toward the door. Angela opened it as soon as he knocked.

"Come on in. I heard your truck pull in. I'm Angela."

"Chase Hodges. I'm sorry about your grandmother. My sister Abby and I used to like to visit her."

"Thank you." Angela didn't bother to explain that she didn't know her at all.

"Your mother actually mentioned that you'd noticed that the roof might need some work?"

He nodded. "After a recent storm, there were a few shingles that blew off and some trim that looked like it was coming loose. Beth said you're hoping to sell soon?"

"Yes, I'd like to. Your mother also gave me the name of a realtor to call, Lauren Snyder."

Chase looked surprised. "Really? She told you to call Lauren?" He quickly added, "Well, she is very good at what she does."

"That's what she said."

"Okay, let's have a look around." Angela walked all around the house with Chase as he examined all the structural areas and made notes on his iPad. They went downstairs into the basement to check the water heater and furnace, and then outside. Chase got a ladder out of his truck and climbed up onto the roof. He walked around and looked under some of the shingles. When he came down, they went back inside and sat at the kitchen table. He clicked a few buttons on his iPad and then turned it around so Angela could see the quote he'd prepared.

He went through it carefully with her.

"The good news is that the roof isn't too bad. You only have to replace and fix a small section of it, where it takes the most damage from storms. I'd replace some of the trim that has come loose or cracked and I'd recommend that you refinish the hard wood floors. That's something that buyers will look for and the less they need to do, the better."

"You think I'd get a better price if I do the floors?" she asked.

"Yes, I do."

Angela did a quick calculation. The estimate was reasonable. She had enough in the local account to cover the repairs and for living expenses for the next few months. As long as she was careful with her spending.

"Okay, let's do it. How soon can you start?"

"I'll have Beth check my schedule for the next few weeks and give you a call. We're finishing up a job at the end of the week and we'll be off the week between Christmas and New Year's Eve, but we should be able to get started soon."

"Great. Thanks so much for coming over so quickly. I really do appreciate it." Angela walked Chase to the door and when she opened it, a pretty woman with a sleek blonde bob was standing there in a stylish dress, high heels and a handbag that Angela knew cost more than her rent had. The woman smiled and held out her hand.

"You must be Angela. I'm Lauren Snyder." She turned her gaze to Chase. "Hi, Chase. This is a nice surprise."

"Hi, Lauren." Chase barely smiled until he looked at Angela. "See you soon." He walked off and climbed into his truck. Angela noticed that Lauren had parked her white BMW sedan right next to it.

"Come on in," Angela said.

Lauren stepped inside and looked around the room, and Angela could see her eyes quickly appraising its worth.

"It's lovely inside. Two bedrooms and a bath on the second floor?"

Angela nodded. "Yes. Would you like to walk around?" She took Angela through the house and she seemed to like what she saw. Lauren used her cellphone to take pictures in every room. When they were back in the kitchen, she asked how the meeting with Chase had gone.

"What kind of repairs did he suggest?"

Angela told her and she looked pleased. "Good. I'm glad you're going to refinish the floors. Buyers love that. Did you have a price in mind?"

"Honestly, I'm not sure. I thought you might have a better idea of the market."

"I do. I know a few buyers that might be very interested in looking at this. It's a good location." She
named a price that made Angela's jaw drop. It was a
little more than what she'd seen online.

"Wow. Okay, that sounds fine."

Lauren fished in her purse and pulled out a business card on thick, pale pink paper. She handed it to
Angela. "Call me when Chase finishes with the work
and then we'll get it listed. It's a slow time of year, but
there are still buyers out there and we'll find them."

"I'll do that."

~

ONCE LAUREN LEFT, Angela took the Mini Cooper for a
drive and spent a few hours wandering all around
downtown Nantucket. She took pictures of the cute
shops and uneven cobblestone streets to send to Jane,
who had never been to the East Coast either. She
decided to take a coffee break when she walked by The
Handlebar Cafe, which looked like a cozy, friendly
place. From looking in the window, she noticed quite a
few people on their laptops and others who had their
dogs with them. Her stomach growled as she saw a
platter of lemon-glazed scones, and she stepped inside.

There was a short line at the counter and as she
waited, Angela debated between one of the lemon
scones or a raspberry shortbread cookie. She went with
a cinnamon coffee and the cookie and as the girl

behind the counter handed over her change, she sensed someone walk up behind her. The girl serving her suddenly smiled from ear to ear and her eyes lit up.

"Good morning. Would you like your usual?"

"Thanks, Bridget. You take such good care of me." The voice directly behind Angela was deep and friendly.

She turned to leave and stopped for a moment. The man waiting for his order was tall and lean. His hair was dark and a bit too long and unruly, tumbling over the collar of his brown leather jacket. He wore a black turtleneck and faded jeans, and was carrying an over-sized laptop. He smiled at Angela and she caught her breath as laugh lines danced around his lips and his very dark, chocolate brown eyes.

"Beautiful morning, isn't it?"

She realized that he was talking to her, and followed his gaze out the window.

"Yes, yes it is." It was unusually warm for the time of year and the sun was shining. She scurried off to a small table by the window, planning to eat her cookie and people watch for a bit before venturing back out. She watched the man who'd been behind her head towards a corner table with his coffee and muffin. He opened up his laptop and inhaled his muffin in just a few bites. He quickly began typing away on his keyboard but every few minutes, he stopped to say hello to people that came in. Many stopped by to chat with him for a few moments before heading to the counter.

She wondered who he was as he seemed to know so many people. But she figured Nantucket was a small place and if he was from the island or had lived there for a while, it made sense that people would know him. She couldn't help thinking that everyone she'd met so far on Nantucket had been so friendly. More than she'd expected as everything she'd read had talked about how people on the East Coast were more reserved and always in a rush.

After Angela finished her coffee and cookie, she ventured out again to do some more exploring. There were so many interesting shops downtown, everything from gift shops with memorabilia and t-shirts to art galleries, jewelry and clothing stores and more. She walked around for a while, and just as she was getting ready to head to the grocery store and then home, a display in a shop window caught her eye. It was a mannequin wearing a gorgeous, pale green cashmere sweater. She knew that she could never afford it, but it was fun to dream.

She walked into the small shop and glanced around. It was full of beautiful dresses, designer shoes and more cashmere than she'd ever seen in one place. Angela had never owned a cashmere sweater. She looked through a rack of sweaters, marveling at the softness and pretty colors. Just as she was about to reluctantly leave to go buy cat food and other necessities, an elegantly-dressed blonde woman glided over to her. Her expression was a bit distasteful, as if she'd seen or smelled something unpleasant. Angela glanced down at her outfit and realized the woman was probably judging her. She'd pulled on an old sweatshirt and faded jeans, and had her hair in a messy ponytail. This other woman was so polished in comparison.

"Is there something you need help with?" the woman asked, but her tone made it clear that Angela didn't belong there.

"No, I think I'm all set. Thank you." She took a step backwards, toward the door.

"We do have a sale rack in the very back, if that might be a better fit for you?" The woman glanced toward the back of the room.

"Thanks, I'll take a look." Angela walked to the sale rack, curious to see if there might be a good deal there. But her jaw dropped when she saw the prices. Even at half off, everything was far out of her price range.

When she turned to leave, the blonde woman was watching her with a satisfied smile, confirmation that Angela did not, in fact, belong in that store. "Have a nice day!"

Angela walked out of the store feeling depressed and a little bit angry. She supposed that she couldn't blame the woman for assuming that she couldn't afford the clothes there based on how she was dressed, but still she didn't have to be so obviously rude about it. Angela was pretty sure that the pretty blonde girl in the store had never had to worry about where her rent was coming from or how to make her money last until the next paycheck.

She shook off her bad mood, though, as she got in the car and drove to the market. She might not have much, but she had enough to buy everything that she needed and she was excited to settle into her new house until it was ready to be sold.

6

L isa puttered around her kitchen, slicing and dicing, and stirring a chicken and wild mushroom risotto. She loved to cook and found it soothing. Every now and then, she glanced out the kitchen window at the ocean. The wind had picked up and the seas were a bit rough with lots of white caps and bigger waves than usual. She didn't mind a good storm, though, as long as the power stayed on and she was inside and warm. They weren't expecting too much tonight, just the wind and maybe a little rain later. She hoped that Rhett would get home before the rain came. The sky was looking darker.

When the risotto was just about done, she shook a generous amount of parmesan cheese over the rice, added a hunk of butter and splash of broth. She stirred everything together and took a taste. A little more pepper and it was perfect. She turned the heat off and covered the pot to keep the risotto warm. Rhett should be along any minute.

Lisa poured herself a small glass of cabernet and settled at the kitchen island with the latest People magazine. She'd just taken her first sip when she heard the front door open and the voice that she loved so much.

"Something smells pretty good!" Rhett came into the kitchen, slid his coat off and gave her a quick kiss hello.

"Thanks. Are you hungry?"

"Starving."

"Pour yourself something to drink and I'll get the risotto. She scooped plenty of risotto into two big bowls and brought them to the island where she'd been sitting. She handed one to Rhett and then slowly sat back down, wincing just a little as she settled onto the stool.

Rhett looked at her with concern. "Your back?"

She nodded. "A few people checked out today, so there was more laundry to do. My back protested a little after having the weekend off."

"I can check with my guy and see if he knows of anyone who might be able to help out." Rhett knew someone that had a network of sorts and was good at finding people for all kinds of restaurant and hospitality work.

"Don't call him just yet. I want to give it a day or two to see if I feel better first."

Rhett didn't look happy to hear it, but simply said,

"All right, then. Just say the word when you're ready and I'll make the call."

"I'll keep that in mind." She reached out and gave his hand a quick squeeze. "Thank you. So, tell me all about your day."

"Well, it was interesting, that's for sure. We were steady, nothing special, but we think we may have had a food critic visit."

"Really? What makes you think so?"

"Just a gut feeling. There were two people and they ordered five entrees between them. The only time I've ever seen that at my other restaurants is when it's a critic that wants to try several dishes for a review."

"That's exciting. Did they like the food?"

"They seemed to. They even ordered dessert." He chuckled. "And there was very little left over."

"I'll watch the paper to see when the review hits," Lisa said.

"Oh, I had a call from your friend Sue today, too. She left me a message about storing sixty or so turkeys in our freezers. Something about a food pantry? She said you suggested calling. I tried her back but didn't reach her."

"I'm sorry. I totally forgot to ask you about that. Abby usually runs the Christmas basket giveaway for our local food pantry, but this year Kate is handling the coordinating. They put together about a hundred boxes with a turkey and everything else to make a nice dinner. The delivery comes in this Thursday and the freezer they usually use isn't available. I thought maybe you'd have some space this time of year?"

Rhett nodded. "We can make room. The extra freezer we use more in the summer has room and there's space in our big walk-in, too. We can make it work. I'm assuming it's just for a week or two?"

"Yes. They put the baskets together a few days before Christmas."

"Tell her to just call me to let me know when they'll be bringing them by. I'll make sure we're ready."

"Thank you. I'll let her know."

"Happy to help. I hate to think of local people struggling to get by, especially this time of year."

7

Angela was a little nervous when she walked to The Beach Plum Cove Inn on Saturday morning. Lisa had said to come around nine and that all three of her daughters would be stopping by for breakfast as well. Angela had decided to walk over, as she'd walked past it the day before as she was exploring the area and it was only about half a mile down the road.

The house was very pretty, big and inviting and right on the ocean, with a wrap-around farmer's porch. She noticed several cars in the driveway and guessed they belonged to Lisa's children. She knocked on the front door and Lisa opened it a moment later, pulling her in for a welcome hug.

"I'm so glad you were able to join us. Come on in. Everyone is in the dining room." Lisa led the way to a large dining room where an older couple was eating bagels and coffee at one end of the table and three women that Angela guessed were Lisa's daughters sat at the other end. Lisa introduced her to Kate, Kristen and Abby, and invited her to help herself to the food that was on a side table. There were big thermoses of coffee, carafes of orange and cranberry juice, bagels and cream cheese and some sort of quiche.

"I splurged a bit today. That's a lobster quiche," Lisa explained.

"If you like lobster, you have to try some. It's amazing," Kate added.

"I've actually never had lobster," Angela admitted as she cut a slice of the quiche and added some fresh-cut cantaloupe on the side. She poured herself a coffee and joined them at the table. Lisa made a plate of food, too, before joining the others. Kate and Kristen were still eating and Abby's plate was empty. She stood as Angela sat.

"I'm going back for seconds."

Angela took a tentative bite of the quiche. She liked Dungeness crab, which was common in San Francisco, so she had a feeling she would probably like lobster, too. The custard was rich and creamy with a hint of nutmeg and some kind of cheese, and the fresh lobster was so sweet. She was surprised that she liked it even better than crab.

"What do you think?" Lisa asked.

"It's really wonderful."

"I made it for Jack when we were dating and he

asked me to move in with him soon after," Kate said with a laugh.

"I'd love the recipe," Angela said. She was usually too busy to cook much between working and school, but for the next few months, she had plenty of time to putter in the kitchen.

"I'll email it to you." Lisa stood to get more coffee and when she sat back down again, Angela noticed that she looked like she was in pain.

Her daughter Kate saw her mother's expression, too. "Mom, is it your back again? I have some Advil if you need it."

"Thanks, honey. I took some just before you got here. It should kick in soon."

"When does Harriet come back?" Kristen asked.

"Not soon enough." Lisa laughed. "Rhett suggested that I look into getting someone to handle the cleaning until she gets back. My back has been really acting up lately."

"You definitely should. Do you know of anyone you could call?" Kate asked.

"Rhett said he could check with someone he knows."

"What kind of cleaning is it?" Angela asked.

"It's just basic cleaning for the five rooms upstairs. Mostly changing the beds when new guests are coming in and stocking the bathroom with towels and soaps, and cleaning the bathtub and floors."

"I'd be happy to do that. I was working as a house

cleaner in San Francisco while going to school. As long as you don't mind hiring someone who is only going to be here for a few months? I was thinking I might want to pick up some work and—well, this could be perfect."

"Really? If you're serious, I'll gladly take you up on it. You could even start today if you like. I can show you where everything is. Unless that's too soon, of course."

"I'd love to. I have no plans for the rest of the day. Or the rest of the month," Angela said with a grin.

"You used to do house-cleaning?" Kate looked interested.

"Yes, for the past four years." She hoped that they wouldn't want to call for a reference, as that would be awkward to explain.

Kate looked around the table. "I had lunch with Philippe the other day and his housekeeper, Judy, is in Florida visiting family for a few months. He mentioned that he'd love to have someone come twice a week to tidy up. Would you be interested? Or would that be too much if you're going to do the cleaning here?"

Angela laughed. "No, it's not too much. I'd love to take on a house or two."

They relaxed and chatted for another forty-five minutes or so. Angela enjoyed getting to know Lisa's daughters. After having met her, she was curious to read Kate's mystery and to stop by the local galleries downtown where Kristen had some of her paintings for sale. She had a feeling they were well out of her price-range, but it was still fun to look.

Abby was closest to her age, just a few years older, but worlds away in terms of where she was in her life—married and with a newborn. Angela had dated different people over the years, but never had a serious relationship. She didn't anticipate that happening until she was out of school and a little more settled in her life.

Abby was very involved with the local food pantry and Angela was impressed to hear what they did for Christmas.

"Sue said that Rhett is going to store the turkeys for us this year. Please tell him I said thank you," she said.

"Oh, he was happy to do it. I won't be able to lift anything this year, but I can sign people in," Lisa said.

"That's perfect. We have a few guys that will be helping to bring the baskets to people's cars and could still use a few people to help pack the baskets. The more the merrier. Makes it go by faster."

"When do you do that? If it's later in the day, I could probably help, too." Angela had always thought about doing some volunteer work and helping with a food pantry appealed to her. She had blurry memories of standing in line at them with her mother when she was very small.

"They will be packing the baskets around five on Sunday, and then passing them out Monday and

Tuesday evening just before Christmas. It doesn't take long to put it all together. "

"My nights are totally free, and I'd love to help with that."

"Fantastic. Just show up at five and Kate will show you what to do. I'm not as involved this year because of Natalie, so I won't be there. Oh, and don't eat dinner. We order a bunch of pizzas for everyone."

∼

ONCE THE GIRLS left and all the food was brought back to the kitchen, Angela followed Lisa upstairs to the five guest rooms.

"Everything you need is in this hall closet, with extra towels and sheets as well as cleaning supplies. The older couple that was eating breakfast has gone out for the day, so we can start with their room."

She opened one of the guest rooms and Angela stepped inside, just staring out the window for a moment. The ocean views were breathtaking. The room was beautifully decorated with snowy white sheets, a pale yellow comforter and navy blue curtains with white trim and shades. Lisa offered to help, but Angela waved her away.

"I've got this. Go relax. I'll bring the linens downstairs when I'm done."

"Thank you. That would be perfect. The laundry room is at the bottom of the stairs."

Lisa headed back downstairs and Angela dove in, making the bed, replacing the towels, cleaning the bathroom and vacuuming. After a few weeks of not working and stressing about finding a job, it was nice to be busy again.

8

The next afternoon at half past three, Angela pulled into the driveway of Philippe Gaston's waterfront home. Kate had texted her the day before to say that Philippe was eager to have her come as soon as she was available to clean and confirmed the time.

She knew nothing about Philippe, other than he was a famous writer and that his housekeeper was away in Florida. She'd gone to the store the night before and bought all the cleaning supplies that she would need. She preferred to use her own rather than the client's. That's the way Happy Cleaners had done it, so Angela thought it made sense to do the same. Plus, there were some brands that she preferred over the ones Happy Cleaners used, so she chose all her favorites and dressed in a pair of jeans and a pale blue sweatshirt with Nantucket across the front of it. She'd bought several at one of the shops along the pier. They were roomy and comfortable, perfect to wear for cleaning. She tied her hair back in a ponytail to keep it out of the way and was ready to go.

When she reached the top step, the front door opened and Angela stopped in her tracks. It was the handsome man from the coffee shop. He was in jeans and a navy turtleneck, his feet bare.

"You must be Angela. I heard your car pull in. Come on inside."

Angela followed him in and he immediately shook her hand. "I'm Philippe Gaston, pleasure to meet you. Kate said nice things. Thanks for fitting me in so quickly."

Angela laughed. "It was easy to fit you in. I have quite a bit of free time these days."

"Kate said you're new to Nantucket? Just here for a few months and looking for a little extra work? Seems like it worked out well for both of us, then."

She nodded. "Yes. I'm not here long and am helping out Kate's mom at the inn. And now you."

"Well, let me show you around." Philippe led her into the kitchen and family room area, and to his office and bedrooms upstairs. The kitchen was the messiest room. Angela smiled at the clutter on his kitchen table and the boxes piled up in the corner of the room, all with the Amazon logo on them. He followed her gaze and laughed.

"I'm a bit of a pack rat it seems. Especially when

I'm deep into the writing of a book. I get out sometimes and go downtown to one of the coffee shops. Otherwise, I'm just holed up here in the kitchen mostly, even though I have a perfectly good office. Judy used to keep me on track before the clutter would get out of hand. Sometimes it's easier to order stuff from Amazon than to go to the store. It probably seems a little crazy to you." He smiled and she noticed deep dimples in both cheeks.

"Not crazy. Just creative. I don't know how you do it, dreaming up stories. It's impressive."

"It's just what I do. I don't know how to do anything else. I'm terrible at cleaning, so thank you for agreeing to help."

"Well, I don't have any creative ability, but I do enjoy cleaning."

"I'll get out of your hair, then. I'm going to run downtown for a few hours and see if I can knock out this scene that is refusing to cooperate. How long do you figure you'll be?"

"At least two hours, probably closer to three. It usually takes me a little longer the first time I clean a house."

"I'll be back before then but just in case, I'll leave you a check now, if you let me know how much." He grabbed a pen and his checkbook. Angela told him the amount. She charged the same that Happy Cleaners would have charged, figuring that the going rate would be about the same on Nantucket. Philippe didn't bat an eye when she quoted him the price. He just wrote it on the check and handed it to her. She folded it in half and stuck it in her pocket.

"Thanks. Good luck with the writing."

~

ANGELA'S CAR was still in the driveway when Philippe returned home a few hours later. He guessed that she was probably almost finished. He hadn't gotten as much work done at the coffee shop as he'd hoped. He was stuck and not sure where to go with his story. He needed to pace around his house blasting Pearl Jam radio until he figured it out. He'd hoped to work all night, but he had that wine dinner with Jessica and though he'd agreed to go, it was the last thing he felt like doing on a Sunday night. Maybe he needed the break and it would help shake loose his ideas.

He let himself into the house and smiled at the sight of Angela in the kitchen, standing high on her toes on a step stool. She was holding a feather duster and reaching into a corner where the ceiling met the wall. It was impressive. He'd never actually seen Judy do that, though he supposed she might have and he just never paid attention. He waited until she noticed him before he said anything so that he wouldn't startle her. She turned and saw him as she took a step down the ladder.

"You're back! I'm just about done and should be out of your hair shortly."

"No hurry at all." He looked around the room and liked what he saw. All the boxes had been flattened and stacked by the door to go out with the trash. His jackets were off the floor and hung in the front hall closet, and the room smelled clean and fresh and a bit lemony. He'd always liked the smell of lemons.

He leaned against his kitchen island and flipped through the mail that he'd grabbed on his way inside. When he looked up, he noticed that Angela was smiling as she scrubbed the kitchen counter. She was humming something under her breath and looked lost in her own world. She was a cute girl, with her almost-black hair pulled back in a ponytail and her pale face with a dusting of freckles across a small, straight nose.

Her light green eyes were the first thing he'd noticed. They were big and stood out against her dark hair. She looked young in her sweatshirt and jeans. He guessed she was maybe just a year or two out of college. Too young for him. Not that he was looking. But he always noticed these things. Cute as she was, though, Angela wasn't his type, anyway. He was usually drawn to the taller, more glamorous types. Angela was maybe five one or two at the most. He was a good foot taller than her.

"What brought you to Nantucket? It's an unusual time to move here," he asked.

"I'm from San Francisco. But my grandmother

recently passed and I inherited her house here. I actually never met her before she died. Isn't that odd?"

Philippe found it intriguing. "Sounds like there's a story there. What did you do in San Francisco?"

"I've been going to school and working full-time, cleaning."

"Full-time? That must be hard with classes."

"It would be impossible, actually. That's why it's taking me so long to get through. I'm twenty-nine, and have been going to school part-time. I just have two more classes to go."

So, she was older than he'd first thought. That was also intriguing. "Then what happens?"

"Well, the plan is to sell the house here, move home, finish school and get a job in marketing. At a tech company probably."

"That sounds like a solid plan. So, you're just here temporarily, then?"

"Probably for three or four months, depending how long it takes to make some repairs and sell the house. I know it's not the best time of year to do that."

"People are always looking to buy houses on Nantucket. I bought this one in January, a few years ago."

"It's lovely. And I hope you're right." They made a plan for Angela to clean again later in the week, and as she walked toward the door, she stopped in front of a framed photograph of the beach at sunset.

"That's beautiful."

He smiled. "Thank you. I took that picture myself, the first time I visited Nantucket. I was here for a vacation and when I left a few weeks later, I knew that I wanted to live here. I bought this house a few months later." And now he couldn't imagine living anywhere else. He traveled to L.A. quite a bit, when one of his books was being filmed, but whenever he wasn't on Nantucket, he missed it. He was hoping that with his new projects, he wouldn't be traveling as much.

9

Angela's cell phone rang as she drove away from Philippe's house and she was surprised to see that it was Kate Hodges.

"I know this is totally last minute, but Jack was supposed to go with me tonight to the Taste of Nantucket event and he's sick as a dog. I thought it might be fun for you, if you feel like going."

"Sure! What is it?" Angela was grateful for the invitation, eager to get out and do just about anything.

"It's a really fun night. Local area restaurants give samples of their food and there are liquor vendors with lots of wines to taste. Kristen and my mother are going, too. Rhett's restaurant is participating."

Angela did a mental inventory of the clothes she'd brought with her and frowned.

"What is the expected dress?"

"It's creative black tie, so almost anything goes. Cocktail dresses, mostly."

"Okay. I'm not sure if I have anything dressy enough to wear. I mostly brought casual clothes with me." She thought for a moment. "Are the shops still open? Maybe I have time to go get something."

Kate laughed. "Don't go shopping just for this. I'm a little taller than you but I think we're about the same size. I have a few dresses you could choose from."

"If you're sure you don't mind?"

"Of course not. Why don't you come by around six thirty? It starts at seven."

~

ANGELA JUMPED in the shower when she got home, fed Sam and arrived at Kate's house at six thirty sharp. Kate introduced her to Jack, who looked miserable. He was laying on the living room sofa, under a blanket, sipping ginger ale and watching TV.

"Nice to meet you. Glad you could take my spot. You'll have a good time. It's always a fun night."

Kate brought her into her bedroom and had three cocktail dresses laid out on her bed for Angela to choose from. They were all lovely, but her favorite was a deep burgundy velvet with a scoop neck and long sleeves. She tried it on in the bathroom and twirled around for Kate to see.

"That looks great on you. It really flatters your dark

hair and light skin. And the shoes are perfect." Angela had brought a pair of simple black patent leather pumps.

Kate was wearing a pretty black and white dress that was sleeveless and showed off her toned arms.

"Okay, we're off. See you later, Jack."

"Have fun!"

~

KATE DROVE and when they pulled up to the country club where the event was being held, Angela was surprised to see that the parking lot was already almost completely full.

"Everyone gets here right when it opens," Kate explained. "That way, you get to try everything before they run out."

After they parked, Angela followed Kate inside and they handed their tickets to the woman checking everyone in. She gave each of them a wine glass and a program that listed all the participants, and also an order form for Bradford's liquors which sold all the wines. They were offering discounts for the evening for those who bought a case or more.

"They will sell so much wine tonight," Kate said as they made their way to one of the wine tables. After a few sips of various pinot noirs, they walked around to see what the different restaurants were offering. There were at least twenty participating and the samples were varied, from lobster rolls and short ribs over mashed potatoes to bite size squares of polenta topped with sautéed mushrooms. There was a lot to try and most of it was delicious.

"There's Kristen and Mom," Kate said as they sampled some cabernet and walked across the room. Lisa smiled when she saw them. She was standing with two other women and introduced Angela.

"These are my two best friends, Paige and Sue. Paige's boyfriend, Peter Bradford, owns the liquor store that is selling the wines and is at one of the booths pouring. Be sure to look for Rhett. He has a booth here too and he's giving out baked scallops and chowder."

"Where's Tyler?" Kate asked her sister.

"He's off talking to Philippe about book stuff. I got bored and went looking for Mom and the girls," Kristen said.

Angela glanced around the room and saw Philippe talking to a handsome man that she guessed was Kristen's boyfriend. Philippe looked sharp, too, in a suit and dark purple tie. She smiled as she looked at his hair. It refused to be tamed and was going every which way, but somehow it worked and he looked great.

"All right, we're going to keep going. Anyone want to come along?" Kate asked.

Kristen shook her head. "I'm really not that hungry. I'll find you guys later."

"You go try everything and report back," Lisa said. "I'm going to find a chair to sit for a bit."

Kate immediately looked concerned, but Lisa saw it and smiled. "I'm fine. Just tired. And I have plenty of Advil with me. Go have fun."

They made the rounds of the restaurant booths, trying so many delicious things. Rhett's scallops were as amazing as Lisa had said, and Angela's favorite was a tuna tartare with avocado from Millie's, a Mexican restaurant. They stopped to talk to Philippe and Tyler, who hadn't moved from where Angela first saw them.

Kate introduced her to Tyler, Kristen's boyfriend.

"Nice to meet you. Philippe mentioned that you cleaned his place today and it looks great. I was thinking about having someone come every week or two. Would you have any time for another house?"

Angela was surprised but quickly recovered. "Sure. Almost any day, late afternoon, is good for me." They traded cell numbers, and confirmed a day and time for Angela to stop by.

"I should probably go find Kristen," Tyler said.

He wandered off and Kate turned her attention to Philippe. "Did you come with Jessica?"

Philippe nodded. "Yes. She's here somewhere. She saw some people she wanted to talk to. Where's Jack? Did he come with you?"

"No. He's home sick. Angela came with me instead."

"Oh, that's too bad." Philippe grinned. "Good for Angela, though. This is a fun event, especially for someone new to the island. What's your favorite so far?"

"Rhett's was good, but I really loved Millie's tuna appetizer."

Philippe nodded. "Millie's is great. It's a favorite with the locals. It's a little off the beaten track, out by the beach. You should go while you're here."

"I will. What did you like best?"

"One of the desserts, a lemon-filled pastry. I love anything sweet and lemony."

"That sounds good." Angela was already feeling full, though, and seldom ate desserts.

"Are your parents coming this year for Christmas?" Kate asked him.

"They are. Usually I go to them, but they agreed to come here this time."

"Where do they live?" Angela asked.

"Paris. They get over to the states a few times a year, though. They love to come in September. The weather is still nice but it's not as crowded with tourists."

"Are you from France? You don't really have an accent," Angela said.

"I was born there and we stayed until I was in elementary school, and then my father was transferred to the states. They lived here for almost twenty years before he retired and moved home to Paris."

"That will be nice for you. Will you cook them something special?" Kate asked.

Philippe grinned. "You know me better than that. I'm having Gary cook us something. He's going to drop it off Christmas Eve and we'll just heat it up. Do you all go to your mom's?"

Kate nodded. "We do. We're going to have a bigger group than ever this year. It should be fun."

"Do you have any exciting plans, Angela?" Philippe asked.

Angela always dreaded when people asked the question, because the answer was always the same. Jane always insisted that she join her family for the holiday and she usually went, but not for long. She just wanted to get through the day as quickly as possible.

"I don't make much of a fuss about Christmas," she said.

Kate and Philippe both looked at her with questions in their eyes.

She sighed and tried to explain. "I don't have any family and grew up in foster homes, so it just wasn't something I ever looked forward to. Especially as it's also my birthday."

Philippe's dark brown eyes grew even darker. "I had a friend who was born on Christmas. He hated it. Said he'd get a Christmas gift from someone and they'd get a funny look on their face and quickly say it was for his birthday, too. He knew they'd forgotten. Was it like that for you?"

"Yes, pretty much. I've never really known anything

different, though. It's just not my favorite time of year," she admitted.

"Well, that really should change," Kate said. "Please spend Christmas with us. Mom would love it and we really do it up. Come Christmas Eve, too. That's when the festivities start."

Angela sighed. "Thank you. But I'm used to spending it alone. I'll be fine." She didn't want anyone to feel sorry for her or as if they had to invite her.

"We'll see about that. I'm going to talk to my mother and she can be very persuasive." Kate had a twinkle in her eye and Angela had a feeling that she might be spending Christmas with the Hodges after all.

∼

LISA HODGES LOOKED around the crowded room as she sipped her glass of wine. She'd tasted a few with the girls, and then just went to the bar and bought a glass of her favorite cabernet. She didn't feel like fighting the crowds all night. Rhett had taken a break and brought her a plate of appetizers, including the baked scallops that were his restaurant's signature dish.

Paige found a table and they were all gathered around it, chatting and people-watching. Lisa was thrilled to see Paige so happy. It had been a long time since her friend had been in a serious relationship, and she and Peter Bradford seemed so well suited. Her friend Sue on the other hand, didn't look nearly as happy. She was her same, bubbly self, but Lisa sensed that something was bothering her. She hoped she was wrong. But if not, she hoped that Sue would share when she was ready.

Kate and Angela joined them and when Angela went off to the ladies' room, Kate leaned over and spoke softly.

"I invited Angela to join us for Christmas Eve and Christmas. It's her birthday. She says she doesn't have any plans and doesn't want to do anything. I think she needs to experience what a real Christmas is like. But you might need to convince her."

"I think I can do that." Lisa knew from their conversation on the plane that Angela didn't have family and there was simply no way she was going to allow that girl to be alone. She thought for a bit and had an idea for how she could approach the idea with her.

When Angela returned to the table, Lisa casually asked if she liked to cook. She remembered that she'd asked her for the recipe for her lobster quiche.

"I do, actually. It's just me, and I was always working and going to school, so I never did a lot of cooking, but I do enjoy it. I was planning to try out some new recipes while I'm here, since I have the time now."

"I wonder if you might do me a favor?" Lisa began.

"What's that?"

"Well, I have everyone over Christmas Eve and

Christmas Day, and I do all the cooking. We have a marvelous Italian seafood feast Christmas Eve and a prime rib on Christmas Day. We have a bigger group than usual this year and the girls help me, of course, by making pies and bringing them over, but I thought if you don't have plans, I could use your help around the kitchen, especially putting stuff in the oven and taking it out. It's the bending that gets me in trouble."

Angela hesitated and Lisa knew she totally saw through the request because of course there were other people who could help. She needed a little more pushing.

"Honestly, I'd just really love to have you join us and it would be a help, if you're up for it?"

Angela smiled and nodded. "Sure. I'd be happy to come."

"Good. Oh, and we all go to the nine o'clock service at the Episcopal church. I hope you'll join us for that, too?"

Angela nodded again. "I haven't been to church in years."

"That's okay. Everyone is welcome and it's a lovely service."

Out of the corner of her eye, Angela saw Philippe walk over. He smiled when he saw Lisa and gave her a big hug.

"Kate tells me your parents are coming for Christmas this year?"

"They are. I'm looking forward to it. Hopefully, the weather will cooperate."

Lisa noticed a look of confusion on Angela's face.

"We often get storms on short notice. If they're particularly bad, the boats stop running and the planes, too. It's one downfall of living on the island if you really need to go somewhere, or get home."

"I never thought about that. We rarely get snow in San Francisco. I wouldn't mind if we get a little," she admitted.

"Me, too," Lisa agreed. "Just enough to be pretty."

⁓

IT HAD BEEN A LOVELY NIGHT. Angela tried just about everything, including so many different wines that it was hard to tell them apart after a while. She was full and feeling a little sleepy by the time Kate asked if she was ready to head home. Philippe was by the door as they got their coats and as they said goodnight, a gorgeous blonde girl ran up to Philippe, wrapped her arms around him and planted a kiss on his cheek. He looked uncomfortable at the display of affection and pulled away. But it didn't deter her a bit.

"This has been such a fun night. Before we go, I want to introduce you to someone." She took hold of his hand to lead him away, but he stopped her and the next thing Angela knew he introduced her to them.

"Jessica, I'd like you to meet two friends of mine,

Kate Hodges and Angela Stark." Jessica smiled and looked at Angela as if she was trying to place her. To Angela's horror, she recognized her immediately as the snooty woman from the cashmere shop downtown.

"You look so familiar. Have we met before?" she asked Angela.

"No. I'm just visiting from San Francisco."

"Oh. Well, nice to meet you both."

"Good night," Philippe said as he walked off with Jessica. Angela watched the two of them go and couldn't imagine what Philippe saw in her, other than her gorgeous exterior. Maybe that was enough.

"She's horrid, isn't she?" Kate said once they were outside.

Angela laughed. "She was so rude to me the other day when I stopped into the shop where she works. I couldn't afford anything there, and she knew it. Philippe seems too nice for her."

"He is. But, she sort of fits his type—tall and beautiful. I wouldn't call him a player, because he's honest with everyone, but he makes it clear that he doesn't want anything serious, with anyone."

"She's okay with that?" Jessica looked as though she thought of Philippe as her boyfriend.

"I doubt it. But she's such a queen bee here on Nantucket, used to getting whatever she wants, and I imagine she thinks that includes Philippe. She may be in for a surprise if he gets wind of her intentions. He generally ends things if he gets the sense things are shifting."

"Well, I think he can do better."

Kate looked at her carefully. "I do, too. I told him just the other day that I hoped he'd meet someone that would make him want more, and he insisted that he didn't think it was possible. He's very charming, but he is quite serious about not wanting to be serious." Angela got the sense that Kate was warning her to be cautious. But she didn't need to. Angela had no intention of falling for anyone on Nantucket as she wasn't planning to stick around that long.

10

I t won't kill me to clean one day a week." Lisa smiled as she lifted her cup of coffee to take a sip. Angela was having breakfast with Lisa and Rhett a few days after the Taste of the Town event. They'd fallen into a routine of Angela coming by a little after eight to have coffee and sometimes a bite to eat before she went upstairs to clean the rooms. She had to wait for the guests to leave first so there was usually some time to kill, and Lisa insisted that she might as well enjoy a hot meal first.

Angela looked forward to the morning conversations and whatever Lisa decided to serve for the day. There was always fresh fruit, bagels and cream cheese as well as one hot item, usually a quiche or frittata of the day. She enjoyed talking to Lisa and Rhett usually joined them, too. He was very protective of Lisa.

"Are you sure that's a good idea?" he asked with a raised eyebrow.

"I'm sure. I've seen the chiropractor a few times now and it's feeling much better. And I've started doing more of that online Yoga to strengthen my core." She looked at Angela. "Have you tried yoga? I'm surprised by how much I like it."

"I like it, too. I used to do some of Adriene's YouTube videos, the beginner ones. I should start doing that again."

"Those are the ones I do. She has a series for lower back pain." She looked at Rhett. "Angela needs at least one day off."

"Okay. But if it bothers you, let me know and we can figure it out."

"I really don't mind, if you need me to pick up an extra day—if your back is bothering you," Angela said. Other than her afternoon cleaning for Philippe and now Tyler, too, she didn't have any other plans.

"I'll let you both know if I need to." Lisa took a bite of ham and cheese quiche and made a face. "I tried a new recipe for this. I think I like my old one better."

Angela looked at her own empty plate and laughed. "I liked it." She'd quickly inhaled every crumb.

"No complaints here, either," Rhett added as he took his last bite.

"Hm. So, has Chase started on your repairs yet?" Lisa asked.

"He's starting today, actually. Said his team would

be over this morning. He's hoping to finish before the holiday."

"That's good. He takes the week between Christmas and New Year's Eve off. I think he and Beth might go up to Killington and ski for a few days. Do you ski?"

"No. I'd like to some day, though. We don't really get snow in San Francisco."

"If you get a chance, you should really explore New England. Killington, Vermont, where they are going, has the biggest ski area on the East Coast. I took lessons there many years ago."

"I would need lots of lessons," Angela said, and laughed.

"They do a great job with lessons. There is a bunny slope—several of them, if I recall. That's where the beginners ski."

"That sounds my speed, if I ever go."

They all looked up as Kristen walked in. By the look on her face, it was immediately clear that something was wrong.

"Hi, honey. Is everything okay?" Lisa asked.

"I just dropped Tyler off at the airport and decided to stop by. I figured you'd all be having breakfast."

"Get yourself something to eat and join us," Lisa said.

"I'm not really hungry, but I will have some coffee." Kristen poured herself a cup and sat across from Angela, next to her mother.

"What's wrong?" Lisa asked.

Kristen sighed. "Tyler's mother just found out that she has brain cancer and it's stage four. He and Andrew are both flying home today. Andrew's going later today, once he lines up coverage for the gallery. They're staying through Christmas, maybe even through New Year's, depending on how she is."

"Oh, how awful. Please give him a hug from me when you see him. Was he very close to his mother?"

Kristen nodded. "They both are. He's devastated and in shock right now. I wish there was something I could do for him, but he needed to go alone. They need to spend as much time with her as they can. It sounds like it's aggressive and she won't have long."

Lisa's eyes watered and she pulled her daughter in for a hug. Angela felt her own eyes get misty, too. Life was so unpredictable.

"I think you were going to be stopping by Tyler's house later today to clean?" Kristen asked.

"Yes, but that's no problem. He can just get in touch when he's back in town."

"Actually, he'd like you to still plan on cleaning today. I have a key so can meet you there. My house is right next door. He was going to wait, but I suggested that he still have you come. He's a recovering alcoholic, so I thought it might be nice for him to come home to a clean house after all this, anything to lower his stress."

"Perfect. I'll plan to meet you there, then." She

agreed with Kristen. A clean house would be soothing for Tyler, and one less thing to worry about.

∾

ANGELA STOPPED HOME after she finished cleaning the rooms at the Inn. Only four of them were rented and everyone went off to explore the island early, so she was able to get in and out fairly quickly. It was just before noon when she arrived home and she was pleased to see a crew of guys there working on the roof. She waved at them as she went inside and relaxed for a bit before she had to head over to Tyler Everly's house at three-thirty.

After a quick peanut butter and jelly sandwich, she decided to do some organizing and cleaning. Her grandmother's house was clean, but there was a lot of stuff Angela needed to go through and decide whether to keep, throw out, or sell.

She started in the small office. The walls were lined with books, most of them in good condition, and some were even leather-bound collector's editions. Her grandmother had clearly enjoyed reading. She also had an old-fashioned Olympia manual typewriter on the polished cherry wood desk. Angela slid a sheet of paper in the machine and hit a few keys. They clanged loudly but left clear ink impressions on the paper. The ribbon was in good condition, which meant it was fairly new.

Apparently her grandmother had actually used this typewriter on occasion.

She leaned back in the soft leather chair and opened the slim top drawer of the desk. There was a pile of letters in it that were unopened and had 'return to sender' stamped on them. Angela looked more closely and saw that they were addressed to her mother. She checked the dates and they were all from before Angela was born.

Her eyes welled up unexpectedly as she found the first letter and slowly opened the envelope. The paper was delicate and yellowed with age. She carefully slid the letter out and unfolded it. The message inside was short and bittersweet.

"Chrissy,

I know we've had our differences and I don't agree with how you've lived your life, especially these past few years, but you are my daughter and my life is better with you in it. It's killing me not knowing how you are or where you are. Please, let me know you are okay. Call me or write to me. I've tried repeatedly to call you, but the number no longer works. I miss you and I hope you know, no matter what, that I will always love you."

Angela's tears fell freely as she finished reading the letter, and she took a deep breath before opening the next letter and the ones after that. They were all similar, with her grandmother imploring her mother to get in touch. The only different one was the last one, written a year after the first.

"My dear Chrissy,

I don't know where you are or how you are and it terrifies me. This is the last letter I will write because it has become apparent that my letters are not getting to you. I kept writing, hoping that they might somehow find you, but if they had, I think I would have heard from you by now. I won't stop trying to find you. If you do by chance receive this, please know that I love you and I want to hear from you, whenever you are ready to get in touch."

Angela slowly closed the desk drawer and sighed. So, her grandmother had tried to reach her mother. She guessed that Chrissy had already moved on before the first letter came. They'd been kicked out of so many places when Chrissy couldn't come up with the rent. What Angela didn't know was what had happened initially. How had her mother fallen out with her grandmother?

Maybe the answer was somewhere in the house, tucked away in another drawer. Or maybe she'd never know? Angela didn't have the energy to keep looking just yet, though. That could wait for another day. She needed to process knowing that her grandmother had tried so hard to find her mother. It was bittersweet knowing that she'd tried and they'd never managed to reconnect.

~

ANGELA MET Kristen at Tyler's house a few minutes before three thirty. After she opened the front door and they went inside, Kristen set the keys on the kitchen counter.

"When you finish up, please lock the door behind you and drop the key off at my place. I'm right next door."

Angela had seen the path to Kristen's house when she arrived. It was just a few steps away, and looked almost identical.

"Our houses are pretty much the same, but you'll see when you stop by later that the interiors are very different. Tyler's is much darker, more masculine. Abby is coming by later, too. You should stay and have a glass of wine with us if you don't have plans? Well, with me. Abby's still not drinking, because she's breastfeeding."

"Thanks, I'd love to."

Kristen let herself out and Angela got to work. Tyler's house was quite a bit smaller than Philippe's so it wouldn't take her as long. It was her first time cleaning it, though, and she wanted to take her time so the house would be fresh and as clean as possible when he returned.

Tyler wasn't as messy as Philippe clutter-wise, but it didn't seem like the house had been dusted or vacuumed in a long time. There was plenty for Angela to do and she spent the next few hours scrubbing until every surface gleamed.

At a few minutes past six, she locked the door

behind her, put her cleaning supplies in her car and walked to Kristen's house. Kristen hollered for her to come in when she knocked. Abby was already there, sitting in Kristen's kitchen, sipping a cranberry and soda water and watching Kristen toss a big bowl of pasta and sautéed vegetables with grated cheese. Whatever it was smelled amazing. She set Tyler's keys on the kitchen table. Kristen glanced up from the stove and smiled.

"Thanks. There's a bottle of red wine open, if you want to pour yourself some. Glasses are in the cupboard by the stove."

Angela did as suggested and settled into a chair next to Abby.

"What are you making?" she asked Kristen.

"It's my famous kitchen sink pasta. I just cooked up all the veggies I had in the fridge and tossed it all together with a little garlic, olive oil and cheese. Please say you'll stay and have some with us. There's tons of it."

Angela's stomach grumbled and she hoped they couldn't hear it. "Sure. It looks wonderful."

Kristen plated up some pasta for each of them and they gathered around her kitchen table. Angela glanced around the room as they ate. Kristen's house did look very different inside. Hers was much lighter and more colorful with some gorgeous paintings, both on the wall and strewn about the room.

"Did you paint all of those?" Angela asked. She

knew that Kristen was a full-time painter, but her work was really breathtaking.

Kristen smiled. "I did. Sorry for the clutter. They're not usually all over the room this much, but I brought some out of my studio to try and decide which ones to bring into town for an upcoming show."

"Did you know Tyler before he bought the cottage next to yours?" Angela asked. She thought it almost seemed like the best of both worlds. To live so close, yet have their own space.

"No, not really. I knew his brother, Andrew. He bought a gallery downtown and we met when I literally ran into his car coming out of the market. There wasn't any significant damage, just a minor scrape, and he suggested that I repay him by bringing some paintings into his gallery. I ended up having a show there that went well and I think we went on a date. We actually had a lot in common, but the timing was terrible."

"She'd just broken up with someone and then decided to take him back," Abby added. It was clear from her tone that Abby hadn't been in favor of that.

Kristen sighed. "It was complicated and I felt I owed it to Sean to give our relationship one last shot. He finally took the step to file for divorce and I thought maybe that meant things would be better with us. But they weren't. And then Tyler moved in. I wasn't even looking for a new relationship then."

"They say that's when it always happens, when you

least expect it." Abby smiled and reached for another scoop of pasta.

"Are you seeing anyone, Angela?" Kristen asked.

"No, I'm very much single. It's just me and my cat, Sam. I'm not really focused on anything serious right now. Maybe after I move home to San Francisco and finish college. I only have two classes left. I kind of feel like my life is on hold until then."

Kristen nodded. "I can understand that. You want to get settled in your career first."

Abby looked thoughtful. "Do you have to go back to San Francisco? You own a home now here. Maybe you could finish your classes online and start a career here. If you like the area, that is? I know living on an island isn't for everyone."

Angela hadn't even considered the possibility of staying on Nantucket. She thought about it for a moment and quickly dismissed the idea. It didn't make sense for her.

"San Francisco is where I'm from, and what I consider home. Even if I did decide to stay here, I don't think there are any job opportunities in my field. Are there any software companies on Nantucket that would need an entry-level marketing person?"

Abby and Kristen looked at each other and laughed at the same time. "Probably not," Abby said. "There are lots of small businesses here, but it's mostly tourism, retail and services. No tech companies that I can think of."

"Oh, well. It was a nice thought," Kristen said as she added a splash more wine to their glasses.

"Have you heard from Tyler? Did he make it home yet to see his mother?" Abby asked.

"He called just before you got here. He'd just seen his mother in the hospital. It's such a sad situation. I'm going to miss him, but I'm so glad that he and Andrew will be with her through the holidays."

"Had she been feeling sick for a while?" Abby asked.

"No, that's the scary thing. She was fine, and had even called Tyler the week before to say she wanted to plan a family trip. A cruise, I think. She had a sudden, severe headache, went to the ER and now this."

"That is scary," Angela agreed.

"It really makes you think. You never know what the next day will bring so it's important to make every day count."

Angela silently agreed, thinking of the day the letter arrived and how her life had changed so much in one day, though fortunately it was for the better, unlike Tyler's poor mother.

11

Philippe almost didn't hear the knock on the door. He was so deep into the scene he was writing that he'd lost all track of time. When he finally heard the knock and glanced at the time, he was surprised to see how late it was—nearly three o'clock, and he knew it must be Angela coming to clean.

His stomach growled as he went to let her in. He'd worked straight through lunch and now that he was aware of the time, he was suddenly starving. He didn't want to lose momentum, though. Normally he'd head out and go downtown but he didn't want to take the time to do that today.

When he opened the door, Angela stood on the front step in her Nantucket sweatshirt, faded jeans that fit her like a glove and her hair in a high ponytail. She smiled when she saw him.

"Did I interrupt your writing?"

He nodded. "Sorry about that. Hope you weren't waiting too long? Time got away from me today."

"Not long at all," Angela said as she walked inside. "I hope it means the writing is going well?"

"Well enough, yes. I hope you don't mind, but I'm going to stay here and hole up in my office. I'll stay out of your way—and don't worry about cleaning that room today."

"Are you sure? I could go through it quick now?"

Philippe hesitated for a second, torn between diving right back in and taking the time to find food and have the room cleaned. His stomach rumbled again.

"That works. I'm going to make a quick sandwich while you're in there."

Angela went off to clean and Philippe opened his refrigerator, staring inside and debating what to have. His eye fell on an unopened package of sliced turkey and the decision was made. Five minutes later, he'd inhaled a turkey sandwich and was on his second handful of chips when his phone dinged with a notification. It was from his agent in L.A. and had the news he'd been waiting for.

P-Good news and bad news. Good first—we got our first choice for the lead—Cameron Davis signed on, which is fantastic. But—he's not available for almost a year, so we'd have to push our start date way out. Let me know if you're okay with that.

Philippe grinned from ear to ear.

He texted back.

"I am very much okay with that. Thanks for the good news."

He was thrilled because it meant no travel for nearly a year.

When Angela finished vacuuming in his office, he was still smiling.

"You're looking awfully happy," she commented as he walked back toward his desk.

"I just got some good news. Looks like I won't have to travel any time soon."

She smiled back. "That's great news. I love to travel occasionally for fun, but I wouldn't like to have to do it all the time for work. I like being at home."

"I do, too."

Angela continued on to clean the next room and Philippe fired up his laptop, quickly getting lost in his story again.

Before he knew it, there was movement outside his office and Angela leaned in to say goodbye.

"I'm all done. I'll see you next Tuesday?"

Philippe stood and stretched. His muscles were stiff from sitting for so long. He was done for the day, too. He'd hit his limit and needed to fill the well to start again tomorrow.

"Yes, we're on for Tuesday. Let me get your check." He opened his desk drawer and pulled out a checkbook, wrote a check and handed it to Angela. His phone chimed that he had incoming mail and he glanced at it. It was a reminder email from the Nantucket animal shelter that one of the two cats he'd looked at was still available. It seemed like a sign that the email came the same day he found out that he didn't need to travel anytime soon.

"What do you think of Mandy?" Philippe turned his phone so that Angela could see.

"Aw, she's so cute! Are you thinking of adopting a cat?"

"I am. Do you think it's a good idea?" He remembered how Jessica had reacted at the suggestion.

Angela nodded. "I'm a cat lover. I have an older cat, Sam, that I adopted years ago from a shelter. He's great company. You should go get her."

Philippe grinned. "What are you doing right now? Want to come along for the ride? Make sure I'm choosing the right cat?"

"Sure. But you really can't go wrong. Shelter cats make the best pets."

She followed Philippe outside, put her cleaning supplies in her car and then hopped into his black Jeep.

"I adopted Oscar, my last cat from the shelter here soon after I moved to Nantucket. He died just a few months ago. I knew I wanted to get another one, but wasn't sure what my travel schedule was going to look like. I didn't want to adopt a new cat, then have to leave it behind for a month or longer."

When they arrived at the shelter, an older volunteer wearing a name tag that said 'Helen' was out front and smiled when she saw them. They told her they were interested in seeing some of the cats. She led them into a big room where there were several cats lounging around and others sleeping. A fluffy, small cat with brown and gray fur and pretty green eyes immediately walked up to Philippe and rubbed against his leg over and over.

Helen smiled at the sight. "She likes you. Mandy's usually a little standoffish with most people. She's five years old and came here a few weeks ago with her daughter. They were left behind when their family moved."

"How can people do that? Animals are family members, too!" Angela reached down to pat Mandy and the little cat rubbed her head against Angela's hand. "She's so sweet."

"Her daughter was adopted immediately, but not as many people want the older cats."

"I'll take her," Philippe said.

"Are you sure? You don't want to look around at all the others first?" Helen asked.

"No, she's the one I came for and it looks like she picked me, too."

Helen led them back out front to process a pile of paperwork and collect a check from Philippe that covered the shots and vet check-up that Mandy had received.

"Did you bring a carrier?" Helen asked.

"No. I can run home and get one, though." He still had Oscar's somewhere in the house.

"I think we might have an extra one. Let me check." Helen walked out back then returned a few minutes later holding a pale blue cat carrier. It was the soft, collapsible kind. Philippe walked out back and looked around for Mandy. As soon as she saw him, she came running. He set the carrier down, opened the door and Mandy didn't hesitate. She strolled right into it, walked in a circle once before she flopped down and began to give herself a bath.

"Well, isn't that something," Helen said. "It's not usually so easy to get them into a carrier."

"No, it's not," Philippe agreed.

"She knows she's going to a good home," Angela said softly.

Philippe looked at her and smiled. Angela understood.

He carried Mandy and her carrier out to the car and they drove home. Once they were back in the house, he set the carrier down and unzipped it. Mandy tentatively stepped one paw out at a time, sniffed the floor, then ran over to Philippe and meowed loudly. He bent down and scooped her up gently. She snuggled against him and began purring.

"Well, it looks like this is a match made in heaven," Angela teased.

He laughed. "Thanks for coming along for the ride."

His cell rang and he saw that it was Jessica. He answered and was about to tell her that he'd call her right back but she didn't give him the chance.

"Philippe, I needed to catch you quickly to let you know I'm heading off island with the girls tomorrow. We're going to Boston. The trip came up suddenly, but I couldn't pass it up. So, I won't be able to go to that lecture thing with you. I'm sure you'll find someone else to go."

"Sure, no problem. Have a good time."

"Thanks. Have to run. Talk later." Jessica ended the call and Philippe just shook his head. He knew that she hadn't been all that excited to go to the lecture with him.

"Sorry about that. Jessica just blew me off for tomorrow night. We're supposed to go to a literary talk, a book signing that a buddy of mine is doing at a local restaurant. She got a better offer to go out with her friends."

~

"SHE DOESN'T SEEM the literary type," Angela said quickly, then immediately regretted the words. She didn't like the woman, but she didn't need to be rude about it.

But Philippe just chuckled. "No, you're right. Jessica's not much of a reader. My friend is a well known writer, too. Jackson Ford."

"I read his last book! It was really good. Does he have a new one out?" Jane had lent her the book after raving about it.

"He does, yeah, and it's already been optioned for a Netflix series. Would you want to come along with me? I have an extra ticket now that Jessica isn't going. It should be a fun night. There will be food and drinks, too."

Angela hesitated for a split second before happily saying yes. She knew that neither one of them saw it as a date, so it was just two friends going out for the night.

"It sounds fun. I'd love to."

"I'll swing by around six to pick you up. Oh, and it's casual. Just let me know your address."

Angela gave it to him and relaxed a bit. She didn't bring any fancy clothes, but she had a few cute sweaters and her favorite slim black pants and boots.

∼

THE NEXT EVENING, at a few minutes before six, Philippe arrived to pick her up. Angela was thrilled to see that it was starting to snow just a little. Swirling flurries of fluffy snow danced in the air before landing.

"Our first snowfall of the year," Philippe announced. "It's actually late. We usually have at least one storm by now. This isn't supposed to amount to much, though."

"It's so pretty. This doesn't happen in San Francisco." Angela was caught up in the wonder of it.

Philippe laughed. "Flurries are pretty. But Nor'easters when the snow is coming down so hard that you can't see more than a foot in front of you, not so much. And shoveling a foot or more of snow, definitely not fun."

Angela climbed into Philippe's Jeep and about ten minutes later, they pulled up to the restaurant where the reading was being held. It was in a back function room and there were about a hundred or so people there already.

"He's lucky this is a good turnout," Philippe whispered. "At my first book signing, only one person showed up. And I was really grateful for that one. It was stressful worrying that no one would show."

Angela had a hard time picturing Philippe in an empty room waiting for readers. His books were so popular.

There was a bar set up in the corner and Philippe ordered drinks for both of them, a beer for himself and a chardonnay for Angela. They found seats as near the front as they could get and waited for Jackson to address the crowd. He'd already waved to Philippe when he saw him, but was surrounded by handlers who were getting water for him and making sure he had everything he needed for his talk.

A few minutes later, once everyone was settled and all the seats were filled, someone from Jackson's publishing company said a few words to introduce him, and then Jackson addressed the group and thanked them all for being there. He was surprisingly funny, considering the dark, moody mysteries that he wrote. Angela enjoyed his dry humor. He had the whole group laughing as he told them about his upbringing, going to a Catholic school and being taught by very strict nuns.

He then moved into reading an excerpt from his newest book. It was the opening scene and ended on a cliffhanger that made Angela want to drop everything and read the book asap.

"He's good, huh?" Philippe whispered.

She nodded. "Is the book out? I haven't seen it online yet."

"I think today is the release day. I'm sure he has some copies here."

He had lots of copies. After the talk, Jackson sat behind a stack of hardcover books and a long line formed of people wanting to buy an autographed copy. One of the handlers took care of selling the books first, while Jackson smiled and chatted with everyone as he signed each book.

Philippe and Angela waited in line, and Philippe bought two books and handed one to her.

"Let me give you some money." Angela reached for her wallet and Philippe waved her off. "I don't want your money. Thanks for coming with me tonight."

"Thank you for inviting me!" Angela accepted the book and handed it to Jackson to sign when they reached him. He looked up briefly, smiled at Angela, then grinned when he saw Philippe.

"Hey, thanks for coming! I'm here for a few more days. We should go out for a beer."

Once the books were signed, they wandered around the room, trying some of the different appetizers and chatting by a big window where they could see the snow falling softly outside. Philippe was charming as he told her funny stories about his experience so far working with Netflix and some of the very popular actors and actresses that starred in the shows based on his books.

"Do you like it better than writing the books?" she asked.

He thought about that for a moment. "No. But sometimes yes. It's very different. The money can be better in TV or film and with TV, you have total control of how the show is created, if you are the show-runner. If you just sell your book to Hollywood and let them do it all, it could end up very different."

"Do you think you'll ever move there?"

Philippe laughed. "To Hollywood? Never. Nice place to visit and occasionally do a project, but Nantucket is home. My agent thought he was giving me bad news that our project has a delayed start date, but it was the best possible news. I'm looking forward to staying here, getting Mandy settled and writing a lot of new books."

"Mandy is awfully cute."

"What about you? Are you eager to get back to San Francisco?"

"I wouldn't say I'm eager. But that's home for me. It's all I know and I am eager to finish school."

"Have you ever lived anywhere else?"

She shook her head. "No. I've only been out of California a few times."

"And now you're on Nantucket. Maybe you'll fall in love with it here and won't want to leave. Like I did."

Angela watched the snow fall outside. It seemed to be going faster and coming down harder.

"I didn't expect to like it so much here," she admitted. "I will miss it when I go home."

"Well, you'll have to be sure and come back to visit, then. Speaking of home, we should probably get going. It looks like it's getting a little nasty out there."

Philippe drove her home and walked her to her door when they reached the cottage. She opened her door and Sam was sitting right there, waiting for her.

"This is Sam," Angela told Philippe as she stepped inside.

"He's a handsome fellow." He bent over and scratched Sam behind his ears, which resulted in immediate and very loud purring, followed by a succession of excited meows as Sam tried to give Angela his opinion on their guest.

"And a character, too." Philippe laughed.

"Thanks so much for bringing me to the signing. It was fun."

"It was, wasn't it? See you soon, Angela."

She closed the door tightly behind her, and went to find a flashlight out and some candles in case the power went out. The winds were picking up, and she remembered that Philippe had said that in Nor'easters the wind often knocked out power lines.

Sam trotted along behind her as she searched the kitchen until she found what she was looking for—an old flashlight and two fat candles that were brand new. If the power went out, she was ready for it.

12

By morning, the snow had stopped and the sun was shining. Angela was grateful that her car was in the garage. She didn't have anything to scrape snow and made a mental note to pick up a scraper at the store, in case she was out somewhere and needed to clean off her car. She started the Mini Cooper and let it run for a few minutes to warm the engine and the inside of the car before driving down the road to the Inn.

She was glad that she didn't have to go far or out onto the main roads, because it was a little slippery. It looked as though the road had been plowed at one point, but there was still a lot of snow and ice packed down. Angela had never driven in snow before and it was a little nerve-racking when she felt the car slide a bit as she turned a corner. She went slower the rest of the way and hoped that the sun would help melt the snow off the roads while she was working.

Lisa and Rhett were drinking coffee when she arrived. She helped herself to a cup and joined them.

"How was the driving out there?" Lisa asked.

"I don't have anything to compare it to. It was my first time driving in the snow, but I just went really slow. It was a little slippery. Very pretty, though."

"I hate driving in the snow. I try to avoid it as much as possible. We heard the weather was going to be bad yesterday, so I stopped at the market and stocked up on groceries just in case we lost power."

"That's a good idea."

Rhett laughed. "The minute there's snow in the forecast, people run to the grocery store and buy up all the water, bread and milk. It can be a little ridiculous."

"If I recall, you were the one that suggested I go to the store." Lisa laughed and Rhett joined her.

"She's right, actually. It's because you mentioned you might make meatballs. I wanted to make sure you had everything you needed."

"Rhett loves my meatballs. I actually made a huge batch of them with sauce. I'll give you a container to take home, Angela. You'll get a meal or two out of them."

"Forecast is looking a little iffy for next week now," Rhett said. He flipped the page of the newspaper that was spread out in front of him.

"What are they saying?" Lisa asked.

"Possible Nor'easter on Christmas Day, though it's still almost a week off, and that could change. Might be sooner, or later, or could go out to sea and we miss it entirely."

"I hope Philippe and his parents are watching the weather. They may want to reschedule their trip. The airport and most definitely the boats won't be running if we get a bad snow storm."

"I'd love to see a big storm," Angela admitted. "But I hope it holds off until after his parents get here."

∼

AFTER SHE FINISHED CLEANING for the day, Angela headed home with a container of homemade meatballs and tomato sauce that Lisa insisted she take with her. The snow had melted and the roads were totally clear, so she decided to stop by the market and stock up on a few things, just in case the weather turned bad again.

She bought a snow scraper and stocked up on pasta, eggs, bread and some chicken. It was so cold out that she thought it might be good soup weather and a batch of homemade chicken soup would last several days.

When she got home and put everything away, she decided to do some more organizing and clearing out of her grandmother's things. She went down to the basement, where she'd noticed a corner of what looked like items in storage. There were several plastic bins and she was curious to see what was in them.

One was full of old shoes and another was baby clothes. They were old and Angela wondered if they had been her mother's. The last bin had an assortment of knick knacks, a few figurines and a big box that looked like it had never been opened. The outside of it said 'soap-making kit'. Angela was intrigued and brought it upstairs to the kitchen table to take a closer look where the light was better.

There was a scrap of wrapping paper stuck to the side and she guessed it had been a gift that was never used. She opened the box, pulled out the instructions and started to feel excited. She and Jane had talked about trying to make their own soap years ago, when Jane got some wonderful-smelling homemade soap for a Christmas gift. But they never got around to trying it.

She took everything out of the box and read through the instructions. It didn't look all that hard. Just a little time-consuming. But she had the time. She gathered everything that she needed and set about following the instructions, heating the oils on the stove until they reached a hundred degrees, and then adding the lye and water mixture and stirring until it thickened and then adding the fragrance.

The kit came with a peppermint scent which sounded good to Angela. She poured half of the white mixture into the mold when it was ready, and after adding a few drops of red color to the rest and stirring it well, she poured the red soap over the white. Then she took a knife and dragged it through in a zigzag pattern to make pretty swirls. Once that was done, she set it aside to rest for twenty-four hours before she could cut it into slices.

It would still be another few weeks before the soap could be used. It needed to cure, ideally for a month. The kit instructions explained that curing was necessary for the water to evaporate and the soap to harden so that the soap would last longer and create a lather better.

As Angela finished cleaning up in the kitchen, she noticed that it was starting to snow again outside and she was very glad that she'd gone to the store earlier. She made some pasta, and heated up the meatballs and sauce that Lisa gave her. Kate called as she was finishing up, to remind her that the Christmas basket packing was that Sunday at the Episcopal church.

"Hopefully the snow will hold off until after we get these baskets packed and given out," Kate said.

THE FORECAST WAS STILL on for a bad Nor'easter for Christmas Day, but the weather was clear the Sunday before when Angela went to the Episcopal church to help put the baskets together. She walked into the church parish hall and saw a flurry of activity.

Kate was at the center of the room, directing everyone. There were about fifteen volunteers gathered, and Angela joined them and helped set up the stations. They piled each long table high with one item that would go in the basket, potatoes, boxes of stuffing, canned vegetables, crackers, apple juice, pies, onions, and cranberry sauce.

"We're just packing the dry goods now. When the clients come to pick up their baskets, they will get a turkey and some butter, cheese and whipped cream. We'll have some of the guys helping outside, handing out the turkeys and carrying the baskets to cars for some of the women or older folks," Kate explained as they piled potatoes on a table.

Once all the tables were full, the assembly began. Everyone took a bright red cloth shopping bag and went around the room, adding one of each item to the bag. With so many people helping, the bags were quickly filled and less than thirty minutes later they had one hundred bags of food lined up along the side of the hall. They cleaned up and then everyone helped themselves to the pizzas that were delivered as they were finishing up.

Angela grabbed two slices of pepperoni pizza and sat with Kristen and Kate. Kate asked Kristen the question that Angela had wondered about, too.

"Any word from Tyler? How's his mother?"

"It's so sad," Kristen said. "They're giving her less than a week now. There's nothing they can do other than keep her comfortable."

"How's Tyler doing with it?" Kate asked.

"He's absolutely crushed. Both he and Andrew are. She's so young, not even sixty. I can't imagine if something like that happened."

"Especially with no warning," Angela said.

"Right," Kate agreed. "Speaking of parents, I was messaging with Philippe earlier today. He's really worried about his parents traveling with this storm coming. If the forecast doesn't change, he's going to have them come the following weekend instead."

"That's a good idea. Even if they managed to get to Logan airport, if there's any kind of a storm, odds are good they won't be able to get here," Kristen said.

"He said he got a cat, too, a cute little Maine Coon, from the shelter. Missy or Merry, I don't remember her name."

"Mandy," Angela said.

Kate looked at her in surprise. "Have you seen her?"

"Yes, and she's adorable. I was cleaning the day that he found out that he won't have to travel next year, and he was so excited that he wanted to go get Mandy right then and there. I went with him. It was really cute how Mandy walked right up to him. Philippe said it was like she picked him, too."

Kate and Kristen exchanged glances.

"Is he still seeing Jessica?" Kristen asked.

"I think so," Kate said. "You know how he is, though. It never lasts long with anyone."

"He is awfully good looking, though," Kristen said. "If I wasn't with Tyler, I might be tempted myself."

"He is a charmer," Kate agreed. "But it would be a mistake to fall under his spell. Philippe is a great friend, but he's a horrible boyfriend. Maybe someday, hopefully, that might change."

~

ANGELA WENT to Philippe's an hour earlier than usual on Tuesday, so that she would be finished in time to get to the church to help Kate and the others give out the baskets.

When she arrived, Mandy raced across the room and seemed glad to see her. Philippe looked on proudly.

"She's so smart. She remembers you from the other day."

"How is she settling in?" Angela asked.

Philippe laughed. "Look at her. She looks like she's lived here for ages." Mandy was flopped at his feet, rubbing her cheek against the side of his shoe.

"She's ridiculously cute." Angela gave her a quick pat before plugging in her vacuum cleaner. Philippe went into his office and closed his door, and Mandy flew across the room at the sound of the vacuum and hid under the sofa. Sam always did the same thing.

When Angela finished vacuuming, Mandy eventually resurfaced and started following Angela around the house, though from a distance. It was very cute. When she was finished except for Philippe's office, she knocked on his door and he brought his laptop out to the kitchen so she could get in to tidy up.

When she was done and went into the kitchen, where Philippe was sitting at the island, she saw that he had the weather map up on his laptop.

"What's the latest on the storm?" she asked.

He sighed. "It's not looking good. I think I'm going to have to insist that my parents postpone their trip a few days. We'll just have to celebrate Christmas the following weekend. I don't think it looks good for them making here for Christmas Eve at this point."

"That's too bad." Angela knew how excited he'd been to host Christmas with them.

He closed his laptop and smiled. "It could be a lot worse. Are you ready to go hand out some Christmas baskets?"

"I'm ready." Angela gave Mandy a final scratch behind the ears before she grabbed her cleaning supplies and stepped outside. Philippe followed her to the church and when they arrived at a quarter to four, there was already a line of clients waiting for their baskets.

"Why do they get here so early?" Angela asked Kate when she unlocked the front door to let Angela and Philippe in.

"I think it's a habit for some of them. The first people in line on food pantry days have dibs on the best meats that have come in that week, before they run out of things."

"Oh, that makes sense," Angela said.

"Philippe, do you want to help Chase carry down the cases of turkeys?" Kate asked.

Philippe went off to find Chase and the turkeys. They brought several cases into the parish hall so that clients would get their bag of food, then grab a turkey on their way out the door.

For the next two hours, they handed out the remaining half of the bags of food and the turkeys. They'd given out the first half the day before. Angela helped out wherever they needed a pair of hands, bringing more bags out, adding the sticks of butter, whipped cream and cheese or helping a client choose a pie. They had stacks of freshly baked pies that had been donated and there was an assortment of flavors— pumpkin, apple, cherry and blueberry.

Lisa and her friend Sue checked everyone in, crossing their names off the list and sending them to Angela and the others to hand out the bags.

Angela's heart went out to the families that came in. Most of them were single mothers with their children. Angela had once been there herself. Though her memories of that time were vague, there were occasional vivid images that stood out, and standing in line with her mother at a food pantry was one of them. Chrissy had always seemed taken by surprise when the holidays rolled around. She was never prepared and their refrigerator was mostly empty.

They'd received baskets like these before and Chrissy had done her best to try to cook the turkey and peel a few potatoes. She didn't always remember to turn on the oven, though, so there was one year where the turkey never happened and while Chrissy was passed out on the sofa, Angela had feasted on an apple pie and nothing else. She hadn't cared, though, at the time, because she didn't really know any different.

"We're going out for our traditional after-turkey-basket drinks," Kate said. "You have to come with us."

Angela laughed. "Okay, if I have to. Lead the way."

They went down the street to Kitty Murtagh's, an Irish Pub that was open year round. There was room at the bar for their small group and Kate opened a tab and took everyone's drink order, and a hot tea for herself. Once everyone had a drink in front of them, Philippe lifted his glass for a toast. "To another successful Christmas basket giveaway. And thanks to Kate for organizing."

They all tapped glasses and agreed that Kate had done a great job coordinating everything.

"How's Jessica?" Kate asked. "I thought you mentioned you were going to see if she wanted to join us?"

"I did mention it to her and she seemed all enthusi-astic, but when it was time to actually help, she was suddenly busy with her friends. They had to go off-island to do some final Christmas shopping."

"Did your parents postpone their trip?" Kristen asked.

"The forecast is pretty grim. I don't think they should risk it at this point. I told them to shoot for this weekend."

"Well, that's too bad," Lisa said. She and Sue were sitting at the bar, sipping cabernet. "Please join us Christmas Eve and Christmas Day, too. We'd love to have you and if you're going to be here, I think I have to insist. Angela is joining us, too. It's going to be fun."

Philippe smiled. "Thank you. I'll gladly accept that invite. I really do appreciate it."

He was standing next to Angela and spoke softly so that only she could hear. "It's not a day to spend alone. I'm glad you'll be there, too."

Angela's first instinct was to explain that she was used to spending that day alone, but thought better of it and just nodded instead. "I'm grateful for the invite, too. It should be a fun day."

"And a little bird told me that it's someone's birthday, too," Lisa said with a gleam in her eye as she looked Angela's way.

"Oh, right, Christmas is your birthday," Philippe said.

"It's nothing. I never make a fuss of it."

"I didn't realize it was your birthday," Kate said. "How fun!"

If she only knew how not fun a birthday it could be. But Angela just smiled and sipped her wine.

"It really will be a good time," Kristen said softly. Angela sensed that she had picked up on her apprehension.

"And the food will be amazing," Kate added.

"So much food," Kristen chimed in. "Though now that Philippe is coming, maybe we should double it," she teased.

"I'm glad we decided to close the Inn for Christmas Eve and Christmas Day," Lisa said.

"Odds are, you would have had cancellations anyway," Kate added.

Angela was glad the Inn was closed, too. The less she had to drive in snow, the better.

"Your car probably isn't all that good in the snow," Philippe said, almost as if he'd read her mind. "Why don't I pick you up on my way over to the Hodges? My Jeep has four-wheel drive and goes through anything."

"Thanks. I was just thinking that I wasn't looking forward to that drive, even though it's not far."

"We'll have all those rooms free upstairs, too, so if the weather is really bad and it's not safe to drive home, there's plenty of room for everyone to stay over," Lisa added.

"I'm still hoping we'll get lucky, and the storm will go out to sea," Kristen said.

Angela was sort of hoping the same, yet part of her was curious about what a true Nor'easter would be like.

As long as she was with other people and not by herself or driving, it might be fun to experience.

"What can I bring for dinner?" she asked Lisa.

"Just bring yourself. And no gifts," she insisted. "None of us need a thing."

But there was no way Angela was going to show up empty-handed. "I'd really like to bring something. How about wine or a dessert?"

Lisa thought for a moment. "We're really all set for dessert, I think. But, I suppose if you want to bring some wine, it won't go to waste."

"Perfect. I'll do that, then."

They didn't stay long at the pub as the next day was Christmas Eve and with the storm coming, everyone had last-minute shopping to do.

As they walked out to their cars, Philippe told her he'd be by to pick her up around six. As Angela drove home, she made a mental list of what she needed to do the next day. She wasn't used to doing much of anything for Christmas Eve or Christmas Day and for the first time, she was surprised to find that she was actually looking forward to it.

13

Angela woke early the next day and over a cup of rich, dark coffee, she made a list of what she needed to get at the store. She also put the weather channel on to get the latest updates on the coming storm. They were still forecasting that it would hit sometime that night and continue all through Christmas Day.

She called Jane to check in and wish her a Merry Christmas and two minutes after she got on the phone, Sam came flying into her lap, wanting her attention. He'd been sleeping in the other room, but as soon as he heard Angela talking to someone other than him, he came running. It always cracked Angela up as it was almost like he was jealous of her giving someone else attention, even if it was just talking on the phone.

"I saw on the news that the East Coast is going to

be slammed with a huge storm. Hundreds of flights have already been canceled," Jane said.

"It's true." She told her about how Philippe's parents rescheduled their trip because it might be too difficult to get to Nantucket.

"The boats stop running, too? That must be so strange. I can't imagine."

"I know. And I drove in snow for the first time. I didn't like it much. The driving part that is. The snow itself is kind of fun."

"Nothing about snow sounds fun to me. Have I mentioned that it's seventy degrees here today? It's gorgeous out."

Angela laughed. "San Francisco really does have great weather. But I have to admit, I'm secretly looking forward to my first big storm."

"Well, don't drive in it!"

"I don't intend do. Philippe is giving me a ride to the Hodges house."

"Remind me who Philippe is? Is he more than a friend?"

"No. Just a friend. He's the one I clean for and he's good friends with Kate Hodges. I've actually become friends with all of Lisa's daughters. And her son, Chase, is doing the repairs on my house."

"How is that going?"

"He's done with the roof and trim replacement. Only thing left is to refinish the floors, but that won't happen now until after New Year's. Pretty much everyone here takes the week between Christmas and New Year's off."

"Could you ever see yourself living there?"

The question took Angela by surprise. "You mean permanently? Or for a vacation?"

"Permanently. You sound like you're settling in."

Angela laughed at the idea of it. "Of course not. It's lovely here and I'd love to come back for a vacation, but San Francisco is home."

"Good. Because I miss you! I am glad that you are excited to go somewhere for Christmas. That's a big step for you."

"I know. It's strange, but I really am looking forward to it. Lisa and her family have been so welcoming."

"Well, I hope you have a very Merry Christmas and a happy birthday. I'll call you after to hear all about it. And be careful in the snow."

Angela smiled. "I will. You have a Merry Christmas, too."

~

SAM WALKED around the living room, flicking his tail back and forth and occasionally pouncing on the curling ribbon as Angela tied it onto the small, clear bags. She'd cut the homemade soap into bars, put one in each bag and tied a red ribbon at the top. The bars needed to cure still but she could just tell everyone to not use them right away. She wanted to do something for the family that had been so welcoming to her. And even though Lisa said no gifts, a bar of soap was just a small thing and it made her feel happy to do it.

She gathered all the wrapped soaps in a tote bag, along with the two bottles of Josh cabernet, the one that she'd noticed Lisa had ordered at the pub. She wasn't sure how everyone would be dressing, but given the weather, she decided against a dress and went with her black pants, a white turtleneck and a soft red sweater that had a white pattern across the top. She'd bought both the turtleneck and sweater at one of the shops downtown a week or so ago when they were both on sale.

It wasn't snowing yet, but when Angela went outside to get the mail, the air had a cold, damp stillness that went right through her. She shivered and hurried back inside. The sky was dark and gray, and she wondered if this was what people meant when they said that it felt like it was going to snow.

She was ready when Philippe arrived a little before six and climbed into his Jeep.

"When are your parents going to come?" she asked as he drove the short distance to the Inn.

"They've re-booked their flights for this Saturday. The forecast looks clear for the rest of the week."

When they reached the Inn, there were already a line of cars parked out front. Philippe parked and grabbed a box from the back of the Jeep.

"What did you bring?" Angela asked as they walked to the front door.

"Lisa said they usually have something bubbly on Christmas Eve, either Prosecco or Champagne, so I brought of few bottles of one of my favorites and Gehricke, a new pinot noir I recently discovered, for tomorrow."

Lisa opened the front door as they reached it and welcomed them in. The rest of the family was already there—Kate and her boyfriend, Jack, Abby and her husband, Jeff, and their baby, Chase and his girlfriend, Beth, Kristen, and Rhett.

"Rhett's daughter was planning to join us, but she postponed her trip to the weekend, too," Lisa said as she took their coats. She thanked them both for bringing wine and had them bring it into the kitchen.

Angela looked around the room and was amazed at how much food there was everywhere. The kitchen island had an array of appetizers—stuffed mushrooms, scallops wrapped in crispy bacon, huge cocktail shrimp, dips and chips and fresh veggies as well as shucked oysters and littlenecks.

"The theme for the night is seafood. We'll have chowder and lobster casserole for dinner and also a tenderloin for those that want some meat as well. Help yourself to everything. What would you like to drink?"

"You said you like to have bubbly on Christmas Eve, so I brought some champagne. We could open a bottle," Philippe suggested.

"That's an excellent idea. Would you like to do the honors?"

Philippe reached into his box and pulled out a bottle of champagne. Lisa's eyes lit up when she saw the label.

"Veuve Cliquot, very nice!"

Lisa got some glasses out and Philippe poured for everyone. They spent the next few hours eating, drinking and laughing. All the food was wonderful, but Angela was especially impressed with the lobster casserole which was full of chunks of fresh, sweet lobster.

"It's the easiest thing in the world to make," Lisa said when Angela asked what was in it. "You just crush up some Ritz crackers, add a lot of butter and a drizzle of sherry. Heat until warmed up and eat!"

"I look forward to this every year," Abby said as she heaped a second helping of the lobster casserole on her plate. "I always go back for seconds but I feel less guilty about it this year."

Her husband Jeff grinned. "She misses 'eating for two'."

Abby laughed. "I really do!"

"The shrimp are really good too," Angela said as she reached for a shrimp and dunked it in the spicy tomato cocktail sauce.

"Those are from Jack's place. The lobster was too, actually," Kate said. Angela knew that Kate's boyfriend, Jack, ran Trattel's Seafood, a family business.

"We set a new record today. I think everyone on the

island must be having shrimp and lobster for the holidays. The line was out the door this morning and we didn't stop until just before closing time, around three."

Angela looked around the room. The kitchen opened into the living area and there was a huge and beautifully decorated Christmas tree by a fireplace that had a fire burning brightly. The mantle was decorated with tiny white lights and boughs of holly. And under the tree, like a beautiful gift, baby Natalie was sound asleep on a snowy white blanket, looking peaceful and adorable in her tiny red velvet dress.

Angela sipped her champagne and felt warm and fuzzy inside as she looked around at all these people who had become friends. She realized that for the first time ever, she was enjoying the holiday. It was a nice change.

"You look deep in thought." Philippe smiled down at her. Everyone else was off in the kitchen, gathered around the island, talking and laughing. A clock above the fireplace showed that it was almost eight thirty, which is when Lisa said they'd be leaving to go to the nine o'clock Christmas Eve service.

"Just thinking that so far this is the nicest Christmas Eve I've ever had," she admitted.

"The first of many, hopefully," he said. "Oh, look up."

Angela glanced up to where Philippe was looking and felt herself blush. They were standing directly under a sprig of mistletoe.

"I don't think we have a choice. It's Christmas law, after all." Philippe grinned as he leaned over and very lightly touched his lips to hers.

"Merry Christmas, Angela."

"Merry Christmas," she said softly. Although it had only lasted a second or two, she'd liked the feel of Philippe's lips on hers. It was unexpected and a bit disconcerting. But it was just a kiss, a mistletoe kiss, so meaningless in the bigger scheme of things.

"Okay, everyone, it's time to head out if we want to get good seats," Lisa called out.

"Time to go." Philippe took Angela's empty glass and brought it to the kitchen sink along with his own.

Angela and Philippe followed the rest of the group to Fair Street and St. Paul's Episcopal church. Lisa led the way inside and found two empty pews in the middle of the church, which was already filling up. Angela had never gone to a Christmas Eve service.

It had been many years since she'd gone to church at all. One of the foster families she'd lived with went every Sunday, and while she lived with them she attended Sunday school, but it was short-lived as she was only with them for a few months. It had left a bad taste as that family had been one of the strictest and least kind of all the families she'd stayed with.

But in St. Paul's as she sat with friends and listened to Christmas carols and a lovely sermon, she felt a sense of joy and hope that she'd never experienced before. And when they stepped outside after the service, it was starting to snow and the flurries of twirling flakes felt magical to Angela.

"See you all tomorrow," Lisa said as they walked to their cars.

It didn't take long to reach Angela's cottage.

"Well, that was a fun night. I'm looking forward to more of the same tomorrow. I'll be by around noon to get you," he said. "Hopefully, the heavy snow won't kick in until later."

"Thanks so much for driving. It was a wonderful night. Drive careful on your way home."

"Will do."

Philippe waited until she was safely inside before he drove off. Angela was still smiling as she scooped up Sam, who'd come running when she walked in the door.

"Maybe Santa brought you something, too," she told him. She had two small stockings hung on the mantle and in Sam's she'd put a fluffy catnip mouse that she'd bought at one of the shops downtown. It was the first time she'd bought stockings, and made any kind of effort for Christmas. She'd seen the stockings and two silvery reindeer stocking holders at the same shop where she bought the catnip mouse. She'd impulsively bought them and they stayed in a bag until she started bagging up the soaps before heading to Lisa's. She'd almost bought a tiny tree as well, but that seemed like too much. Now she was wishing that she had, after seeing how beautiful and full of light Lisa's tree was.

Angela took another look out the window at the falling snow before changing into her softest flannel pajamas and climbing into bed. For the first time ever, she didn't feel stressed about the holidays and fell into a happy, deep sleep almost as soon as her head hit the pillow.

14

The snow stopped during the night, so when Philippe arrived a little before noon to pick Angela up, the roads were clear and the air was damp and cold, but there was not a flake to be seen yet.

"It's definitely coming," Philippe said. "I can feel it in my bones, literally. I broke my leg skiing years ago and whenever bad weather is on the way, my leg aches."

"Your parents made the right decision postponing, then. Although it doesn't really seem too bad. We only got a dusting of snow last night."

Philippe laughed. "Just wait. I'm going to remind you that you said that later."

Everyone was at the Inn except for Kate and Jack, who were spending the day with Jack's family and, if weather permitted, Lisa said they would try to stop by later in the day. She had her new grand-child, Natalie in her arms and the baby was adorable.

"I told them to play it by ear, and to stay safe. They were here last night, so I told them to just relax and plan to spend the day with Jack's family. We can see them the day after."

"I always loved the day after Christmas," Kristen said. "We'd just spend the day playing with all of our new toys."

"And eating all the leftovers," Chase added.

"I always love it, too," Lisa added. "It's a relaxing day, nothing to rush around for."

"If this storm is as bad as they predict, there won't be anywhere to rush off to," Rhett said.

"It doesn't look like it's going to amount to much," Abby said as she looked outside. The wind had picked up some and the trees were blowing but there was still no sign of snow.

"That's what Angela said earlier, too," Philippe said with a chuckle.

"Anyone ready for a little coffee cake and a mimosa?" Lisa offered. She had a cinnamon walnut coffee cake on the island next to a pitcher of mimosas and glasses.

After everyone had a slice of cake and a mimosa or coffee, they spent the next few hours watching *It's a Wonderful Life*, a holiday classic that Angela had never taken the time to watch before.

"This is Mom's favorite, and it's a tradition to watch it together every year," Kristen explained.

By the time the movie ended and the bell rang announcing that Clarence had received his angel wings, Angela's eyes were damp. It really was a wonderful, uplifting film. Philippe was sitting next to her on one of the sofas. As the credits rolled, he turned to her and said, "Now that is good storytelling."

When the movie ended, Lisa went to the Christmas tree and picked up a box wrapped in red paper with a big white bow on top. Much to Angela's surprise, she handed to her. "I know we said no gifts, but this isn't a Christmas gift, it's a birthday gift."

Angela was speechless. Other than Jane, who always made a point to give her a birthday and Christmas gift, no one else ever had since her mother died. Chrissy at least had always remembered and always gave her what she could, usually something small. Angela opened the box and gasped as she pulled out an absolutely gorgeous cream-colored fisherman's knit sweater. The yarn was soft and the pattern was beautiful with intricate cables all over it.

"Thank you so much." Her eyes fell on the tag inside the sweater, which read, 'Made with love, Lisa'. "You didn't actually make this, did you?"

Lisa nodded and Rhett added proudly, "She knits constantly, while watching TV or talking to me. I don't know how she does it."

"I love to knit. It relaxes me and it was a pleasure to

make it for you. Now you'll look like a real New Englander."

Angela stood and gave her a hug. "Thank you so, so much."

Kristen handed her another box. "This is from the three of us. We noticed that you don't have some necessary winter apparel."

Angela opened the box and smiled as she saw a bright red knit hat, and matching mittens and a scarf.

"Thank you. I really do need these, all of them."

"Last but not least, I got you a little something, too." Philippe handed her a heavy box and Angela wondered what it could be. She opened the package carefully and drew out a leather bound, signed special edition of Philippe's first and most popular book. Angela had admitted that she hadn't yet read any of his books.

"Thank you. I can't wait to read it." She got up and found the tote bag she'd left there the day before and handed out her little plastic bags tied with the red ribbon. She'd curled the ribbon so it fell into spirals and looked festive.

"I thought we said no gifts," Lisa protested as Angela handed her one of the soaps.

"It's just something little and you can't actually use them for a month. They still need to cure."

"You made these?" Kristen sounded impressed.

"I found a soap-making kit in the basement and it was something I'd always wanted to try. It was really fun, actually, and I want to make some more with different colors and scents."

Abby held hers to her nose and inhaled deeply. "It smells wonderful, like a candy cane. Next time you make soap, please let me know. I'd love to do it with you."

Philippe smiled as she handed him his soap. "Thank you for this. I'll have to hide it from Mandy. She has a thing for ribbons. I caught her chewing on one when I was in the middle of wrapping some gifts."

"Sam does the same. I think it's a cat thing," Angela said.

"Look, the snow is here." Angela followed Lisa's gaze out the window and sure enough, snow was falling, fast and furious.

"I'll get some more wood for the fire." Rhett stood and went into the garage and returned a few minutes later with an armful of wood and set it by the fire.

"I hope the power doesn't go out," Angela said. The snow looked fierce and the wind was howling outside.

"Doesn't matter if it does," Kristen said. "Mom has a generator. My parents installed it years ago and if the power goes out, it kicks on automatically."

"I'm very glad we put that in," Lisa said. "Especially now that we have guests staying here. It's fun for about five minutes when the power goes out and then the thrill wears off fast."

Angela and Kristen helped Lisa in the kitchen and

took several hot dishes out of the oven. Rhett took the rib roast out and set it on the counter to rest while Abby brought the serving dishes to the table. Philippe opened two of his bottles of pinot noir and poured a glass for everyone that wanted one. There was roasted asparagus, mashed potatoes, creamed spinach, and Yorkshire pudding popovers and honey butter to slather on them.

Rhett carved the roast and put the slices on a platter so that everyone could help themselves. Once everyone had a full plate, they settled in the dining room and enjoyed a delicious dinner with good company. Everything was good but the popovers, which were as light as air and melted in her mouth, were Angela's favorite.

The lights flickered a few times while they ate and the storm intensified. They could hear the wind howling even more loudly as it roared in off the ocean.

"Usually, being this close to the water means that we don't get as much snow. It just blows away, but a Nor'easter is different. You never know where the wind will blow," Chase said.

"At least we are up high enough that we've never had to worry about flooding," Kristen said. Lisa's house was set back from the beach and had a staircase with about twelve or so steps down to the water level.

When they were just about done, the lights flickered again and then they heard a whirr of something and

Abby said, "The generator just kicked in. I wonder how many have lost power?"

"I imagine it will be most of the island, if this keeps up," Rhett said.

"Well, I'm glad we're all here, and safe," Lisa said. "Unless this storm stops soon, I think everyone should plan to stay over. There's plenty of room, no sense driving in this weather, especially with the power out and possibly lines down on the road. The winds can be brutal."

No one protested. It was clear that the storm was only going to get worse. They put the news on and watched the storm coverage for a while. The whole East Coast was getting a Nor'easter and cancellations we're rolling in. The boats and local airport closed earlier and even Logan was almost completely shut down. Angela was fascinated and she'd never seen anything like it before. The storm was expected to wind down sometime during the night but total expected snowfall was close to two feet in some areas.

"We have Paul Thompson set to come plow us out in the morning," Lisa said. "He comes automatically if we get more than a few inches of snow."

"We'll all be out there shoveling our cars out, though," Rhett added.

"Enough talk about snow," Kristen said. "I'm already sick of winter. Philippe, what is Jessica doing for Christmas? What did you get for her gift?"

Philippe looked slightly uncomfortably, Angela

noticed, as he answered the question.

"She's spending it with her parents. I got her a nice bottle of wine and gave it to her yesterday at lunch. I'm not sure she liked it all that much, to be honest."

Abby looked intrigued. "Do you think she was expecting something else? Jewelry, maybe, possibly a ring?"

Kristen laughed at the idea. "She's not very bright if she expected a ring."

"I think she might actually have expected jewelry, and ideally a ring. I thought we were on the same page with this relationship, but it doesn't seem that we are. She was also expecting to meet my parents and I told her that wasn't likely."

"Why not?" Angela asked.

"If I introduce someone that I'm dating to my parents, they will expect it to be someone I'm serious about. I don't want to get their hopes up or set the wrong expectation with someone."

"How did she take that?" Kristen asked.

"Not well. She told me we're done, and she took back my Christmas gift."

"She did? What did she give you?" Abby asked.

"A titanium Apple Watch. It was really nice, but she said she wasn't going to waste it on me if I wasn't looking to take things to the next level. I'm not sure what made her think that I would be. I try to be so clear with people." Philippe looked so perplexed that Angela almost laughed.

"You didn't do anything wrong," Lisa said. "One day, you'll find yourself so head over heels for someone that you'll be excited to introduce her to your parents."

Philippe smiled. "Kate said something similar to me recently."

"So, you're on the market again? I'll have to warn all my friends," Abby teased him.

"I'm not in any hurry to rush back out there," Philippe laughed.

They relaxed over coffee for a while and when everyone was ready, Kristen and Abby brought out the pies they'd made earlier in the week.

"We usually get together at Kate's and make three pies—an apple, a pumpkin and a blueberry. Mom likes us to stay out of her way in the kitchen, so this is our way of helping."

"It works out perfectly," Lisa said as she cut herself a slice of blueberry pie.

Once everyone had their fill of dessert, Abby and Angela helped to clear the table while Kristen got a deck of cards and they spent the next few hours playing a rousing game of pitch, a game Angela hadn't played before. Philippe helped her during her first few rounds until she got the hang of it. It was a fun game and Angela quickly learned that the Hodges family was very competitive but it was all in fun.

Later that evening, Lisa brought out a platter of sandwiches and Angela was surprised to find that she was hungry again. They all were and everyone collapsed in the living room to watch another Christmas movie. This time it was the Will Ferrell comedy *Elf*, a movie that Angela had seen before and loved.

By the time the movie ended, everyone was yawning.

"I think I'm going to call it a night," Lisa said. "Angela and Kristen, why don't you girls take the room that has the two beds, and the rest of you can decide amongst yourselves on Tyler. Angela knew from cleaning them that all the rooms were about the same size except for the one with two double beds, which was a little bigger.

Everyone headed upstairs. Angela and Philippe were the last in line and as they passed out of the living room, Philippe laughed and stopped under the mistletoe again. He looked down at her and smiled. "It's the Christmas rules, remember?"

"So it is." Angela was feeling happy and sleepy and a little curious to see if Philippe's second kiss would be as good as his first.

It was—though like the first, it only lasted a few seconds.

"Merry Christmas and happy birthday, Angela."

~

THE NEXT DAY, Angela looked outside her bedroom window to see a blanket of white everywhere. The snow had stopped, the sun was shining and it was really beautiful.

Kristen was awake, too, and when they went downstairs, Angela saw that Philippe and the other guys were already outside shoveling the cars out. Lisa had hot coffee ready and they gathered around the kitchen island, drinking coffee and eating leftover coffee cake.

When Philippe and the others came back inside, Angela asked how deep the snow was.

"We have about a foot, I'd say. Maybe a little more in some places," Rhett said. "The wind blows it all around. They probably have a little more inland."

"Do you know if you have any snow shovels at your place?" Philippe asked.

"I think I saw a few in the garage," Angela said.

"When I drop you off, we'll get your driveway shoveled out then. It's a short one, so it won't take long. It's better to do it now, while the show is light and fluffy. It will get harder the longer it sits there."

"Oh, okay. I guess we should do that, then. Thank you." It hadn't even occurred to Angela that she might need to shovel snow. It wasn't something she'd ever done before.

"Well, if you want to get your car out of the garage and go anywhere, it will help." Philippe grinned.

"It looks like the plows have been by. The road actually looks pretty good," Jeff said. "I think Abby, the baby and I are going to head out."

"We should go, too," Philippe said. Angela

grabbed her coat and after they said their goodbyes, Philippe helped her to carry her boxes out to the Jeep.

It didn't take long to drive the short distance to Angela's cottage and as Philippe had said, her driveway was a blanket of snow about a foot tall. They trudged through the snow with her packages and once they were inside, they went into the garage, got the shovels and after Angela put on her new hat, mittens and gloves, she helped Philippe shovel out the driveway. By the time they finished, about twenty minutes later, her muscles were protesting and her cheeks were frozen. She invited Philippe to come inside and warm up before he headed home.

"I can make us some coffee or hot chocolate. What sounds good to you?"

"Hot chocolate for me, thanks. Oh, hello there." Sam looked like he'd just woken up from a nap as he slowly strolled into the kitchen and immediately went over to Philippe and sniffed his leg, then rubbed against him.

"Sam's twelve. He doesn't act his age though. He thinks he's still seven." Angela handed Philippe a mug of hot chocolate and made one for herself as well.

"Oh, you made the good kind, with the little marshmallows."

"Is there any other?" Angela laughed.

They went into the living room and settled on the sofa.

"I'm lucky that I didn't lose power here," Angela said.

"You lost power. I noticed your coffee machine was blinking. You are lucky that it's back on, though. I hope mine is, too. Unlike the Hodges, I don't have a generator. Though now that I've seen one in action, maybe I'll get one."

"What are you going to do today, write?" Angela asked him.

"Probably. My parents aren't due to come for a few more days still, so I might try to get ahead so I can take time off when they're here. What about you?"

"I think I might make a big pot of chicken soup. I bought all the ingredients earlier in the week, but ended up making soap instead and put the chicken in the freezer."

"It's good weather for homemade chicken soup. I'm a little jealous, actually. I wasn't smart enough to go shopping before the storm. I don't have much in the house, other than peanut butter and jelly. I suppose I could have that."

Angela laughed. "Well, if you feel up for it, feel free to come by later for dinner. I'll have plenty of soup."

"Maybe I will. I do have plenty of wine. I could bring a bottle as my contribution."

"I won't say no to that."

Philippe stood. "All right. I'll get out of your hair, then. I'll plan to stop by later, maybe around six or so?"

"That's perfect."

15

After Philippe left, Angela showered and then puttered around in her kitchen, chopping onions and celery and peeling carrots and potatoes for the soup. Her grandmother had an Instant Pot just like the one Angela had once had in San Francisco and sold when she had her eviction sale, as she thought of it. The Instant Pot made it so easy to make good soup fast. Angela just dumped the bone-in split chicken breasts in, added the vegetables and enough water to cover it all then she just pushed the button that said poultry and let the pot work its magic.

Her phone rang a moment later and it was Jane calling to wish her a happy birthday and to find out how she was managing in the big storm.

Angela told her all about it, right down to shoveling out her driveway.

"A foot of snow? I can't even imagine what that would be like. And Philippe gave you a Christmas gift?"

"No, a birthday gift."

"Really? That's so nice. Didn't you say he had a girlfriend? Was she there, too?"

"No. And it sounds like they're not dating anymore."

"Oh? How interesting. He sounds like a great guy. Maybe you should go for it," Jane suggested.

"It's not like that with us. We're just friends. Philippe is a great friend but according to everyone, he's not an ideal boyfriend. To be fair, he never claimed to be."

"Oh, that's too bad. Although if you were to fall for him, you might not want to come back here. When do you think you'll be coming home?"

"Probably not for a few more months. I still have to list the house, sell it, wait for it to close and get the money and then I'll be back."

"What are you up to today?"

"Making a big pot of soup and being lazy. Philippe is coming for dinner later and I thought I'd just watch movies this afternoon. What about you?"

"Well, it's gorgeous here, so we're getting takeout and then watching movies, so not too different. Interesting that Philippe is coming for dinner. You're sure there's nothing going on there?" Jane sounded so suspicious that it made Angela laugh.

"No. He just heard I was making soup and invited himself over. He said he'd bring wine, so I said okay."

Jane laughed, too. "Okay, then. Well, enjoy your day and keep me posted on when you're coming home."

"Will do."

~

ANGELA SETTLED on the sofa and pulled a soft, fleece blanket over her. She searched Netflix for a good movie and decided on a classic one she'd seen many times, *When Harry Met Sally*. She loved the story of two friends that eventually realized they were meant to be together. Sam jumped up onto her lap and they watched the movie together. Angela put another one on after, but soon found herself falling into a nap. She slept for over an hour and only woke when her phone dinged. It was Philippe.

"Hey, I'm just checking in to make sure you still want company for dinner? I'm going to head over in about twenty minutes or so, if that works for you?"

Angela glanced at the time. It was already almost six. And after being around a houseful of people the past two days, Angela's house felt very quiet. Too quiet.

"Yes, I'd love your company. Come over anytime. Soup's ready."

She jumped up and went to check on the soup. It was done and keeping warm. She pulled out the chicken breasts, shredded the meat and returned it the pot. She added a pinch of salt and pepper. She changed out of her comfy sweats into a pair of jeans and a sweater, and ran a brush through her hair. Sam ran to his food bowl, so she fed him and got two soup bowls and napkins out.

Ten minutes later, there was a knock on the door. Angela let Philippe in and his face was red from the cold. He handed her a paper bag and a bottle of wine.

"I wasn't sure if you needed bread, but I have this loaf that I picked up the other day." It was a crusty sourdough and Angela knew it would be perfect with the soup. She set it on the kitchen table, got some butter out and found her wine opener. Philippe opened the bottle, which she noticed was the same pinot noir he'd brought for Christmas. He grinned when he saw that she recognized the label.

"I may have bought a case of this wine after trying it at the Taste of the Town." He poured a glass for both of them while Angela put a block of cheddar on a plate and found a box of crackers.

"I thought we could have some cheese and crackers first, with the wine. Unless you're starving and ready for soup?"

Philippe laughed. "I'm in no rush."

"Did you get much writing done today?"

He laughed again. "Not a word. I had all the best intentions but once I stretched out on the sofa, with Mandy sleeping at my feet, my eyes closed and I was out for a few hours. I didn't even try to write after that."

"I did the same. It was a nice, lazy day."

"What are you planning to do with your parents when they're here?"

"They just want to relax and go to some of the restaurants they haven't tried yet. We might fly into Boston for a night or two and see a show. They love to see live theater or the symphony, and my mother will want to go to the Museum of Fine Arts. Maybe do some shopping in the Back Bay."

"That all sounds wonderful."

"Have you been to Boston yet?"

"Only Logan airport so far."

"You should try to get to Boston while you're here. It's a great city, easy to walk almost everywhere."

"Maybe I'll do that, if I get the chance. I'm not sure how much longer I'll be here."

Philippe frowned. "That's right. I keep forgetting that you're only here temporarily. Maybe you should come with us, then?"

"With your parents?" Angela remembered how he said he didn't want to introduce Jessica to them.

"Yes. They love meeting my friends." Angela relaxed at the word friends. She was glad they were on the same page. Philippe was becoming a good friend. She just wouldn't think about the way his lips had felt on hers.

"Are you ready for some soup?"

"Sure, why not?"

Angela ladled soup into the two bowls while Philippe sliced some bread. They settled at the kitchen table and enjoyed the simple meal.

"This might be the best chicken soup I've ever had," Philippe said and Angela laughed.

"Thank you, but it's really nothing special. It's very easy to make. There's a ton of it. I'll send some home with you."

"I'll gladly take it."

After they finished eating and everything was put away, Philippe added a little wine to their glasses. They went into the living room and sat on the sofa, which faced the fireplace. The two stockings were still hanging there, but Sam's was empty. Angela had given him the catnip toy and it was a big hit.

"What's in your stocking?" Philippe asked.

Angela grinned. "Dark chocolate-coated caramels from the candy store downtown. It was my little treat to myself. Would you like one? I think I'm going to have one."

"Sure."

Angela got up, handed a chocolate to him and popped one in her mouth as she settled back on the sofa.

"Is that a wood-burning fireplace?" Philippe asked.

"Yes, I think so. I saw a pile of wood in the garage. I haven't tried to use it yet, though. I was afraid I might do it wrong and set the house on fire."

Philippe laughed. "I can show you how, if you like. It is perfect weather for a roaring fire."

"Sure. If you don't mind."

"I'll be right back. I remember seeing that wood in the garage, too, now that you mention it." He stood and returned a few minutes later with an armful of wood and set a few logs in the fireplace. He showed Angela how to open the flue to vent the smoke to go up the chimney. He found some newspaper, crumpled it and set it on top of the logs.

"That will help the logs catch fire," he explained as he lit the paper with a match. A few minutes later, there was a small fire, which grew to a crackling one and quickly sent warmth their way. They settled back on the sofa and Angela stared at the fire, watching the flames dance and enjoying the warmth.

Philippe clicked on the television. They watched the news for a bit and the continuing storm coverage. Many other areas of the state were still out of power and had up to three feet of snow in some areas. They decided to watch a suspense movie on Netflix that neither of them had seen yet. It was good, and the time flew by as they sipped their wine and the fire glowed merrily. Angela was enjoying Philippe's company and was glad that he'd practically invited himself over for dinner. It was much nicer than eating alone every night with Sam.

By the time the movie ended, they were both yawning and the fire was dying out.

"I should probably get going. I need to be up early tomorrow and have a productive day."

"Do you still want me to come by to clean?" Philippe hadn't been home long enough to mess it up since the last time she'd cleaned just a few days ago.

"Yes, definitely. My parents will be here the next day, so I'd like the place to be as spotless as possible. My mother is a bit of a neat freak."

Angela smiled. "All right, then. I'll see you around three tomorrow." She got up to walk him to the door. Sam followed them and sat waiting for someone to give him attention. Philippe was happy to oblige and leaned over to scratch him behind his ears. Sam flicked his tail and arched his back, encouraging Philippe to keep going.

"Thanks for dinner. I will enjoy this tomorrow." Angela had given him a container of soup to take home. He pulled her in for a hug, and then was on his way. Once he was gone and Angela closed the door behind her, her place felt so quiet without Philippe's energy. She yawned again. It had been a busy couple of days.

"Come on, Sam. Let's go to bed."

16

Whenever Judy, his regular housekeeper, used to come and clean, Philippe almost always left the house to get out of her way. He liked to go downtown and write in coffee shops sometimes anyway. Writing was an isolating job and as much he loved immersing himself in his story world, Philippe was also an extrovert. He liked being around people and knew he was bound to run into people he knew if he spent a few hours at the coffee shop. He didn't usually mind the interruptions. It was more of a welcome break.

But since Angela had started cleaning, he wasn't as eager to leave. There was something about her that he really liked. She was easy to be around. Maybe it was because he knew they were destined to just be friends. She'd made it very clear that her stay on Nantucket was limited. And she was such a total opposite to Jessica that it was a welcome breath of fresh air.

It was also fun to be around her as she experienced snow for the first time and going to church for Christmas Eve service. She didn't talk about it much, but he knew her life hadn't been easy. Growing up in foster care must have been rough. He admired her dedication to keep working toward her degree and her willingness to work while she was on the island.

His phone rang and a moment later, Mandy hopped into his lap and circled around twice before plopping down and looking up at him expectantly, waiting for him to pet her. He did as he answered the phone warily. It was Jessica calling and he wasn't sure what she wanted.

"Hey, there. Merry Christmas!" he said.

"Right. Same to you. I'm calling to invite you to my New Year's Eve party."

Well, that was unexpected. "Oh, well, I'm not really sure about that. I think my parents might still be here."

"The ones you didn't want to introduce me to?" Jessica whined.

Philippe didn't know what to say to that.

"If I'm able to, I'll try to stop by," he said to appease her, and then yelped as a set of small teeth clamped onto his hand.

"Mandy!" The little cat jumped off his lap and walked off, flicking her tail back and forth.

"Who is Mandy?" Jessica asked.

"My new cat. She just bit me."

"I don't even know what to say to that, but I'm not surprised. That's what cats do."

"Right." Philippe rubbed his thumb while Mandy glared at him and Jessica chatted on about nothing in particular. It was almost as if she'd forgotten that she'd said she was all done with him. Why did women have to be so confusing? Even girl cats gave him a hard time.

There was a knock at the door and Philippe knew it was Angela.

"I have to go. Angela's here."

"Who is Angela?" There was a sharp tone to Jessica's voice.

Philippe sighed. "She's a friend and the woman who is cleaning for me while Judy is away."

"Oh. My cleaner just quit. Could you see if she might be interested in cleaning my place, too?"

"Sure, I'll ask her. I don't know if she is looking to take on any new clients, though."

"If she's running a cleaning business, she'll be interested. Just ask her, please."

"Will do."

Philippe went to let Angela in. Mandy followed along behind him and ran right to Angela when she walked in.

"Hello, you cute thing!" Angela bent down and scooped her up. Mandy, traitor that she was, snuggled against Angela's chest and purred so loudly that Philippe could hear it from where he stood.

"Women!" Philippe said.

Angela laughed as she set Mandy down. "What happened?"

"Mandy was on my lap, happy as could be, until I started talking to Jessica and then she bit me!"

"Jessica bit you, or Mandy?" Angela teased him.

"Mandy, but I wouldn't put it past Jessica, either. She called to invite me to a New Year's party, as if everything was fine and we'd never had words the other day."

"Are you going?"

"No! I'm not planning on it. Plus I think my parents might still be here. I'm not sure."

"Did you tell her that?"

"Well, yes, sort of. I did tell her I'd try to make it if I could."

Angela just raised her eyebrows and said nothing.

"I know. It was just easier to do that."

"No wonder Mandy bit you." Angela laughed.

"Oh, and here's the best part. I told her I had to go because you were here to clean and she asked me to have you call her. She's in the market for a new cleaner, evidently. I told her I didn't know if you'd be interested but I'd pass the word on."

Angela surprised him by immediately saying, "I'd be happy to clean her place."

"You would? Really?"

"Sure, why not? I might as well make as much

money as I can while I'm here, right? Besides, it gives me something to do."

"Okay, if you're sure. She might be somewhat difficult."

"I'm used to difficult."

Philippe jotted down Jessica's number and handed it to Angela, who tucked it in her pocket.

"All right. I'm ready to get to work."

"I'll go hibernate in the office."

Philippe got quite a bit of work done in the next few hours while Angela cleaned. He found the background noise of the vacuum cleaner oddly soothing, like white noise. Mandy, on the other hand, felt differently and came running into his office for protection at the first sound of the vacuum. She let him pick her up and she was trembling. All was apparently forgiven and now she loved him again.

"Silly girl," he said and let her snuggle against him. Eventually, she relaxed and went to sleep on his lap and he lost himself in his story again.

He was so into his story world that he was startled at the sound of a knock on his office door. He looked up as Angela peeked inside and smiled.

"I'm all done everywhere else. Do you want me to do your office now?"

He looked around the room. It was still spotless from the last time she cleaned and he didn't want to upset Mandy with the vacuum again.

"I think we can skip it today." He stood and went

out to the kitchen. He wrote out a check for Angela and handed it to her.

"Thanks again. If you're interested, Kate just messaged me that she and Jack and Kristen are going to the movies. There's a new comedy that looks pretty good. It just opened today. Show is at seven."

"Sure. Where should I meet you?"

"I'll swing by and get you a little before seven."

Angela smiled. "Great. See you then."

Philippe closed the front door behind her as she left and was surprised by how happy he felt that Angela had agreed to go to the movies with him. They were just friends, so it was surprising how much he was enjoying spending time with her. He tried not to remember how much he'd enjoyed the feel of her lips, too. Mistletoe kisses weren't real ones, though. Certainly nothing to take seriously. Even if Angela was interested, he'd be hesitant to date her. He liked her too much as a friend to start a romance that could never have a happy ending.

~

WHEN ANGELA GOT HOME, she pulled out the slip of paper that Philippe had given her and called Jessica. She answered on the second ring.

"This is Jessica!"

"Hi, Jessica. It's Angela Stark. Philippe gave me

your number and said you are interested in having your place cleaned?"

"Yes, thanks so much for calling. I'm home tomorrow morning, if you'd like to come by. My condo is the furthest one out on the docks. You can't miss it." She rattled off the exact address and Angela jotted it down.

"I'm working in the morning. But I could come by around three, if that works for you?"

"I suppose that will have to do. See you tomorrow." Jessica ended the call before Angela even had a chance to say goodbye. She smiled and shook her head as Sam walked across the room, meowing loudly.

"Someone's hungry," Angela said as she opened a can of food for him. She hoped that she hadn't made a mistake by agreeing to clean Jessica's house. She'd agreed mostly because she was curious about the woman and because she could use the money. Until she sold her grandmother's cottage and cashed the check, she needed to watch her spending. Taking on cleaning jobs could help ease her ever-present fear of running out of money.

∾

ANGELA JUMPED IN THE SHOWER, dried her hair and dressed in the pretty sweater that Lisa had made for her. She paired it with her favorite jeans, a turtleneck and boots. She had a bowl of leftover chicken soup and froze the rest as there was still quite a bit left.

Philippe knocked on her door at exactly a quarter to seven and they set off for the movie theater.

"Are you excited about your parents' visit? What time do you expect them tomorrow?"

"I am looking forward to it. As long as they don't have any delays, they should be here around this time tomorrow."

"Will you still do your big Christmas dinner for them?"

"Yes. Gary dropped everything off earlier today. All I have to do is heat it up tomorrow."

"Will you tell your parents you made it?" She teased him.

He laughed at the idea. "They know better than that."

Kristen, Kate and Jack were at the theater waiting for them when they arrived. Philippe bought tickets for Angela and himself, and she insisted on buying the popcorn and drinks. The movie was a good one and after it finished, they walked to the Irish Pub for a drink. They all agreed that it was one of the better romantic comedies that they'd seen.

Kristen was quieter than usual and Angela asked her if everything was all right.

"Everly's mother passed yesterday. So, I didn't get a lot of sleep last night. I'm actually heading out day after tomorrow to go to the wake and funeral. Tyler's going to stay a few more days with his father and then he'll be home."

"Oh, I'm so sorry."

"Thanks. It's really awful. I think it's hitting Tyler and Andrew really hard. But, how could it not, right?"

"Right."

Angela excused herself to go to the ladies' room, and while she was in the stall, she heard a familiar voice.

"No, I'm not back with him yet, but I'm working on it. I invited him to my New Year's Eve party."

"Is he coming?" an unfamiliar voice asked.

"He said he'll try. His parents are in town, so I'm not sure. But, either way, we'll get back together. I'm not letting him go that easily."

"He does have a reputation. Maybe he won't settle down with anyone."

"I'm not worried about that. I just underestimated how long it would take. I didn't get a ring this year, but I will next year. Just wait."

They both laughed, while Angela couldn't believe what she was hearing. Jessica was delusional. Or was she? Maybe she could eventually win Philippe over. He had almost agreed to go to her party, after all.

When Angela came out of the bathroom, she wasn't surprised to see Jessica talking to Philippe. Angela walked over to where Kristen and Kate were standing. Kristen and Kate exchanged glances when Angela reached them. "You should go over to

Philippe," Kate said. "Make it clear that you're with him, so she'll go away."

Angela laughed. "I don't think so. We're not together like that. Besides, maybe he wants to get back together with her. He can do whatever he wants."

Kristen sighed. "We just don't like her. He's too nice of a guy to tell her to beat it."

About ten minutes later, they were all happy when Jessica and her friend said their goodbyes and left the bar. Philippe quickly came over to join them. His eyes found Angela's. "I'm so sorry for that. I tried to tell Jessica I was here with friends, but it took her a while for it to sink in."

Angela thought about telling him what she over-heard in the bathroom, but decided against it. He'd find out soon enough what she was up to. And it was up to him to decide what to do about it. Suddenly, Angela was very tired and just wanted to go home and go to bed.

Luckily, Kate and Kristen were yawning too and when they finished their drinks, they paid their tab and headed home.

"Have fun with your parents tomorrow," Angela said when Philippe pulled into her driveway.

"Thank you. And good luck with Jessica. Remember, it's not too late to say no!"

17

W hen Angela arrived at the Inn the next morning for coffee, Lisa's friend Sue was there instead of Rhett. Angela poured herself a coffee and joined them.

"Angela, you've met my friend Sue, I think?"

"Yes, we met at the church for the Christmas basket giveaways."

"Where's Rhett today?" Angela asked. He was always there, every morning that Angela had been.

"He had to go off-island this morning and took the early boat. He's meeting with a new supplier."

"How are you enjoying Nantucket?" Sue asked. "Lisa said you're only here for a few months, until you sell your grandmother's house?"

Angela nodded. "I'm liking it here more than I expected. I didn't know what to expect, though. It's a beautiful place, and the people are so friendly." She smiled at Lisa.

"You could always decide to stay, and just live in your grandmother's cottage," Lisa suggested. "We love having you here."

"It is tempting, but I could never afford to live here," Angela said.

"How much money do you need? You own your cottage outright. Real estate taxes on Nantucket are the lowest in the state, and you're already building a cleaning business," Lisa said.

Angela laughed at the idea. "I'm filling in for your regular person and I've picked up a few odd jobs cleaning. I don't think that's enough to support myself."

"You're majoring in marketing, right? You could use what you've learned to market your own business and find new clients."

Angela smiled. "I've been cleaning houses for years now. I went to college to do something else."

"It was just a suggestion. You do seem to enjoy the work, and if you build it up, a cleaning company could be a good little business."

"I've never thought about that before. I was planning to work for a software company."

"And that's a good idea, too." Lisa turned her attention to her friend. "Speaking of growing a business, how is your new girl working out? What's her name again?"

"Brandi. And she's great. She's about fifteen years

younger than us, blonde and drop-dead beautiful. If I wasn't so secure in my marriage, I might be worried having her work so close to Curt every day, but I really like her. And business is up since she started."

Angela smiled. "Speaking of beautiful, I did agree to take a new client on. Philippe's ex-girlfriend, Jessica, wants me to clean her condo. I'm going over later this afternoon to meet with her."

Lisa looked less than thrilled at the news.

"Oh, honey, are you sure you want to do that? She seems like she could be a handful. I've heard she's not the nicest person to work for."

"Who is she?" Sue asked.

"Jessica Lavin. Her family is one of the richest on Nantucket and she manages one of their stores downtown. It's full of overpriced clothes that the average person could never afford."

Angela smiled. That summed up how she'd felt about the store perfectly.

"I've worked for plenty of difficult people over the years. I think I can handle Jessica."

"I have no doubt that you can. But why would you want to? Don't let her give you a hard time."

"I won't," Angela promised. She thought it was sweet that Lisa was so protective of her.

"I'll want to hear all about it tomorrow," Lisa said.

∾

JESSICA'S CONDO was at the end of a long pier and was about as 'on the water' as you could get. Angela double-checked that she had the right unit number and then knocked on the door. No one answered, so Angela waited a moment and then knocked again, louder. Just as she was about to knock for a third time, the door swung open and Jessica stood there with her cellphone glued to her ear. She motioned for Angela to come in and turned around and walked away.

Angela followed her into the kitchen and waited while Jessica finished her call.

"I don't care that you're closing at six, I need you to finish my dry-cleaning by then. I have an event to go to tomorrow. I'll be by just before six. Fine, goodbye." She ended the call and spun around to face Angela.

"Most places have such horrible customer service these days, don't you agree?"

Angela said nothing, sensing that Jessica wasn't done yet.

"I mean, I dropped my dry-cleaning off this morning and they don't want me to pick it up until Monday. That's ridiculous. I need it today. They said something about being short-staffed, but that's not my problem, right?"

"Hm," Angela said.

"Anyway, crisis averted. They said they'll do their best to have it ready for me. So, you're a friend of Philippe's? He said you do a great job cleaning his place."

"Yes, he's great. I met him through Kate Hodges."

"We've dated a bit, but he says he doesn't want anything serious," Jessica said. "Is he dating anyone else that you know of? I mean, have you seen any other women there?"

Angela shook her head. "No, it's always just him and his cat, Mandy."

Jessica made a face. "I told him not to get a cat. Horrible creatures. Did you know his cat bit him? What kind of a pet does that?"

Angela tried not to laugh. Mandy was smarter than anyone realized.

"Anyway, let me show you around." Jessica gave her a tour of the condo and it really was lovely. There were two big bedrooms, three bathrooms and a spacious living room and kitchen that had huge, oversized windows that looked out over the water. It almost felt like they were on a boat the way the water surrounded them.

"Have you lived here long? Your views are so beautiful."

Jessica beamed, pleased by the compliment.

"Thank you. It was a present from my father on my twenty-fifth birthday. He thought it was time that I had my own place."

Angela didn't know what to say to that. She couldn't imagine having the kind of wealth that resulted in being given such a gift at such a young age. At any age, really. And the condo was beautifully decorated, too. Jessica had exquisite taste. There were plush, winter-white sofas and ocean blue throw rugs, accent pillows and knit throws in soothing neutral shades. The overall effect was one of comfortable elegance.

The bedrooms were just as beautiful, and there was also a small office that was spotless and looked as though it had never been used. The master bath counter was piled high with all kinds of beauty products and Jessica's walk-in closet was bursting with gorgeous clothes, many of them still with the price tags on them.

When they finished the tour and were back in the kitchen, Jessica wrote out a check and put it on the counter.

"Well, I'm going to head out. When you finish up, please just make sure the door is locked and pull it shut behind you. I'll be in touch in a few days to see about scheduling your next visit."

"Okay. Thanks, Jessica." Angela was eager for her to leave so she could get started. Jessica's place was fairly neat, so it shouldn't take too long. Once she left, Angela put her music on and started cleaning. Two hours later, she was completely done except for Jessica's office, which didn't need much more than a little dusting and a quick vacuum. As she was about to leave the room she noticed the screen on the desktop and did a double-take. It was Angela's LinkedIn page which showed her online resume and most recent employer, Happy Cleaners. At first, it gave Angela an uneasy feeling, but then she shook it off a moment later and figured Jessica was just checking her out and obviously was fine with what she saw there.

~

ANGELA ENJOYED A QUIET WEEKEND. Abby invited her to hang out Sunday afternoon while Jeff was off with his friends watching football. They ordered pizza and ice cream, and had a Hallmark movie marathon. Abby still hadn't lost her baby weight but didn't really seem to care. She was exhausted while their baby slept by fire while they watched the movies. They also ordered soap-making supplies from Amazon and selected several different scents. Once Angela received everything, they were going to have a soap-making party as Kate and Kristen had said they'd be interested in trying it, too.

On Tuesday, just as she was about to head out the door to clean Philippe's place, her cell phone rang and she was surprised to see it was Nora from Happy Cleaners calling.

"Hello?" Angela couldn't imagine what Nora wanted.

"Angela? It's Nora from Happy Cleaners. How are you?"

"I'm fine, thanks." She didn't feel like making small talk with the woman that had fired her.

"I owe you an apology. I knew in my gut that you couldn't have possibly stolen that bracelet."

"Oh? Did she find it?"

"Sort of. Her daughter Julia is in rehab now for heroin addiction. She confessed that she stole the bracelet to get money for drugs. I just wanted to let you know and to offer you your job back, if you're still interested and even living in the area? I also had a call from someone checking a reference on you, from Nantucket of all places."

"Was it Jessica Lavin?"

"It was. I told her you'd been fired, but also told her it was all a terrible mistake and that I'd love to have you back. You were one of our best cleaners. I hope it's not too late." So, Jessica had actually called Happy Cleaners. That was surprising.

"Well, I am in Nantucket, but it's temporary. I'm hoping to be back in San Francisco in a few months."

"When you're ready, just give me a call, then. And again, I'm so sorry, Angela."

~

ANGELA FELT bad that Julia was suffering from the same addiction that Chrissy had struggled with. She wouldn't wish that on anyone. She was glad and relieved that she'd confessed about the bracelet. It had been a horrible feeling to be accused of something she hadn't done and to be fired for it. It was also a relief to know that when she did go back to San Francisco that she could start working right away. She wasn't in a hurry, though, as she was enjoying her time on Nantucket, and wasn't eager for it to end.

When she reached Philippe's house, she could hear a flurry of activity and voices even before he opened the door to let her in.

"Angela! Come in. Meet my parents, Miriam and Pierre Gaston." She shook both of their hands and in heavy French accents, they both said they were happy to meet her. Philippe looked very much like his father. They had similar dark hair and eyes. Philippe was just a few inches taller. His mother was lovely. Like most French women, she seemed effortlessly beautiful and stylish. She was wearing a black turtleneck sweater and tailored, charcoal gray pants. Her hair fell in a sleek bob to her chin and her eyes were a pretty blue-gray. When she smiled, her whole face lit up.

"Have you had a nice visit so far?" Angela asked.

"Yes, we love Nantucket. Philippe has been a very good host. He cooked for us and has taken us to several of his favorite restaurants."

"Where did you go?"

"Millie's for tacos and the Brotherhood of Thieves for burgers. It was delightful."

Philippe grinned. "We're going to kick it up a notch and go out in Boston New Year's Eve. My mother wants the chocolate cake at Abe and Louie's."

She nodded. "He said it's the best. And I do love chocolate."

"I'm trying to get tickets for Hamilton," Philippe said.

"Oh, I heard that is amazing," Angela said.

"They've been sold out for weeks, but my ticket guy is trying to find a few for us. Fingers crossed."

"Good luck," Angela said as Mandy came running over to her. She reached down and patted her.

"She likes you," Miriam said.

"She loves Angela," Philippe said. "She was with me when I got Mandy from the shelter."

His parents exchanged glances but said nothing.

Angela wasn't sure if they were planning to stay or go off somewhere. "Where would you like me to start?" she asked.

"Oh, anywhere. We're heading into town and will be back in a few hours. If you finish before we get back, your check is on the counter."

"Are you going shopping?" she asked.

"Maybe. But I think we're going to go through the whaling museum first. They haven't seen it yet." The whaling museum was down by the pier, and was one of the first things Angela had explored when she arrived and had some time to kill. It was fascinating seeing the history of the island.

"Oh, you'll love it. I found it very interesting," she said as they headed toward the door.

A few hours later, just as she was finishing up and about to leave, Philippe and his parents returned.

"Oh good, you're still here," Philippe said when he saw her.

"I was just about to leave. Did you have fun at the museum?"

"You were right, dear. It was fascinating. We stopped at a coffee shop and had a cappuccino and a scone."

"I got a call with some good news, too. My ticket guy found some great tickets to Hamilton, third row center."

"Oh, that's wonderful! You'll have a great time."

"There's one catch, though. They only sell the tickets in pairs. So, I had to take four of them, which means I have one left over. Any interest in joining us?"

Angela's jaw dropped. "You want me to come with you to see Hamilton?" She wasn't sure what to say. It seemed like so much. She knew tickets to a show like that were very expensive and it was in Boston, with his parents. She really wanted to go, but she hesitated, not sure if it was a good idea or not.

Miriam put her hand on her arm and smiled. "Come with us, dear. It should be a fabulous show and we're going to go to the Museum of Fine Arts in the afternoon, then have dinner before the show."

"You'll have your own room at the hotel," Philippe said. "It really should be fun. Say you'll come with us."

Angela was about to say yes, then realized that she couldn't possibly go.

"I'd love to, but I can't just take off on Lisa. She's depending on me to clean the rooms at the Inn.

Philippe grinned. "That's already taken care of. I checked with Kate and Kristen and they said they'd be happy to cover for you for a few days."

Angela was blown away. He'd thought of everything.

She smiled. "All right, then. Thank you. I guess I should see Boston at least once before I go back to San Francisco."

Philippe's eyes seemed to darken.

"Yes, you definitely should see Boston at least once."

18

The trip to Boston with Philippe and his parents was a wonderful whirlwind. Philippe called an Uber to drop them at the Nantucket airport and they flew straight to Boston. It was a gorgeous day, sunny but cold. They took another Uber to the hotel to check in and Angela was suitably impressed to see that it was the Four Seasons, which was many steps above any hotel she'd ever stayed in.

They had several suites reserved, on the same floor —a bigger one that was more like an apartment for his parents, and smaller, one-bedroom suites each for Philippe and Angela. Angela thought it was extravagant to get suites for all of them.

"A regular room would have been fine for me," she told him as they dropped their bags in their rooms, which were really lovely. Angela's had a pretty view of Boston Common and the gardens.

"It wasn't an option. The only available rooms they had were the suites because we booked so last minute." He grinned. "It's all good, though. My accountant says I need the tax write-off."

They spent the afternoon exploring the Museum of Fine Arts. Angela especially enjoyed the Downton Abbey exhibit as she'd watched every episode, and the Monet watercolors, which she'd always thought were gorgeous.

They had a delicious dinner at Abe and Louie's, a steak house on Boylston Street in the heart of Boston's Back Bay Area near the historic Copley square and all kinds of shopping at the Prudential Center. Miriam and Angela both had the chocolate cake for dessert. It was six layers high and Philippe and Pierre ended up helping both of them because it was so massive and amazing.

They walked over to the theater after dinner and it felt good to move around. The tickets were waiting for them at the theater and the seats were incredible. They were so close that Angela could see beads of sweat on one man's forehead. The show was every bit as good as she'd heard and as they walked back to the hotel, they saw fireworks in the sky the entire way.

"It's First Night festivities, fireworks and all kinds of activities like face-painting, at Boston Common," Philippe said. They decided to walk over since it was so near the hotel and Angela was amazed at the size of the crowd. It was almost as if all of Boston was out celebrating.

They didn't stay too long, though. Miriam was tired and Angela found herself yawning, too. It had been a long day but a wonderful one.

When they reached the hotel, Philippe asked if they wanted to have a nightcap in the Bristol Lounge before heading up to their rooms. His mother smiled and shook her head.

"No thanks, honey. We're exhausted. You kids go have a glass of champagne and toast in the New Year. We'll catch up with you in the morning for brunch."

"What do you think? A little champagne sound good?" Philippe asked.

Angela smiled. It was already eleven thirty, so it wouldn't be long before the ball dropped and ushered in the new year.

"Of course. Lead the way." She followed Philippe into the Bristol Lounge and they slid into two seats at the bar that opened up as they walked in.

"Perfect timing," Philippe said.

A moment later, the bartender brought over a silver dish with hot, salted nuts and took their drink order. When they both had their glass of Veuve Cliquot, Philippe lifted his and said, "To your first Boston visit."

She tapped her glass lightly against his and smiled. "Thank you for including me and for making it so special."

"It's my pleasure. It's fun playing tourist and seeing things for the first time through your eyes."

Angela glanced out the window. Fireworks were still going off and it was almost midnight.

"They are coming on Monday to refinish the floors. That's the last step before I list the house with Lauren. I wonder how long it will take to sell?"

Philippe smiled. "Are you in a hurry to get back to San Francisco?"

"No, I'm actually not in a rush at all. It's been so much nicer than I expected, meeting you and the Hodges family. I won't mind if it takes a little longer. Since I've picked up a few cleaning jobs, my money is lasting longer, too."

"Well, selfishly, I hope your house takes forever to sell." He grinned and Angela laughed.

They both turned toward the television where the countdown was happening. They watched the ball drop in Times Square and all around the bar, couples kissed to celebrate the New Year.

"Happy New Year, Angela." Philippe leaned over and brought his lips to hers. This time, it was a real kiss and lasted for more than just a second. When it ended, Philippe looked as dazed as Angela felt.

"Happy New Year," she said softly, and then yawned as the long day caught up to her.

"Ready for bed?" Philippe took the last sip of champagne and she did the same. They were both quiet as they rode the elevator up to their rooms, which were adjacent. Philippe waited until she had her door open before he walked off.

"See you in the morning."

Angela changed into her pajamas and climbed into bed. Her head was spinning as she replayed the kiss with Philippe over and over. It had been wonderful and terrifying at the same time because she understood now how easily it could be to fall for him. He was handsome and fun to be with, but he was dangerous, too, because of his track record.

It would crush her to fall hard and have Philippe pull back when things got too serious. It was his pattern and there was no reason to suggest that it would be any different with her. So, it was best not to let it happen again, and just stay friends. And Philippe had become a good friend. She didn't want to lose that.

~

PHILIPPE WAS CONFUSED by his feelings for Angela. They had developed a strong friendship, yet when he kissed her, he didn't want to stop. But he knew himself too well and he didn't want to ruin their friendship by being his usual non-committal self. He still didn't see that changing any time soon. And he knew Angela was still determined to move home to San Francisco, so starting anything romantic just didn't make sense. At least if they stayed friends, he could see her if he went to California or if she visited Nantucket, and he was pretty sure she'd be back for a vacation and to see the new friends she'd made, including him.

Angela acted as if they'd never shared a kiss the night before when he saw her at brunch, and he took his cue from her and did the same. His mother raised her eyebrows, though, as she looked at both of them, and then she smiled slightly. Philippe suspected she really liked Angela and he hated to get her hopes up that there could be anything more than friendship between the two of them.

After a relaxing brunch at the hotel, they took a walk across Boston Common to the North End and stopped at Modern Pastry. Philippe's mother wanted to get some cannoli and nougat candy to bring back to Nantucket. They checked out of the hotel, took a cab to the airport and flew back to Nantucket, arriving mid-afternoon.

Philippe had an Uber waiting for them when the plane landed and they dropped Angela off on the way back to his house. As soon as Angela said her goodbyes to his parents and to him, his mother let him know what she thought of her.

"She's lovely. What are you going to do about it?"

Philippe laughed. "Nothing. She's a good friend and she's moving across the country. San Francisco is home to her."

"Home can be anywhere you want it to be," his mother said.

"Well, I'm glad you both liked her."

"Eventually, my dear, you need to stop all this playing around and grow up a little."

Philippe's jaw dropped. His mother had never spoken to him like that before. He looked at his father, who just shrugged and stayed silent.

"It's just that we love you, honey, and we want you to be happy."

"I am happy, Mom. I have a wonderful life."

"I'm glad you're happy, honey. So, what shall we do tomorrow?"

19

S am was sound asleep when Angela walked through the door. There was also a package from Amazon on her front step. She brought it inside and set it on the kitchen table. The soap-making supplies had arrived. Once she was unpacked and settled in, she messaged Abby and her sisters to see if they wanted to come by that Saturday afternoon for a soap-making session, and maybe have pizza and wine after. She also had a message from Jessica asking if she could come and clean on Monday.

She spent the rest of the day doing laundry and running errands, stocking up on wine for when the girls came over, soda for Abby and a few groceries and cat food to get her through the week.

It was nice to have a few days off from cleaning and when she arrived at the Inn the next morning, Lisa and Rhett were both eager to hear about her Boston trip.

"I heard that Hamilton is just wonderful. I tried to get tickets to go with the girls when the show was first announced, but they sold out so fast. Unless you go through a special ticket reseller and pay astronomical amounts."

Angela laughed. "I think that's what Philippe did. And they only sell in pairs so that's how I got a lucky invite."

"And you went to Abe and Louie's, too. Did you get the chocolate cake?"

"Yes, and it really was wonderful."

Lisa sighed. "The first time I went there I was with friends and before we ordered, we saw several of them go by and I knew that was what I wanted. I almost didn't even care about my dinner. I just wanted to get to dessert."

"Where did you stay?" Rhett asked.

"The Four Seasons. I'm not used to staying at such a posh place."

"Well, it sounds like you had a wonderful first visit to Boston."

"I did. We walked over to the North End, too, to Modern pastry and I had my first cannoli. I may be addicted."

"There are no bad bakeries in the North End. Some people prefer Mike's. We like Modern, but it's all good. What did you think of Philippe's parents?"

"They're nice. Philippe looks a lot like his dad, but

has more of his mother's personality, I think. His father is very quiet and lets his mother chatter away."

"How long are they staying?" Lisa asked.

"I think they're flying home tomorrow."

"Are you still planning to go back to San Francisco?" Lisa asked.

The question surprised Angela. "Yes, of course. They are coming on Monday to refinish the floors and then the house will be ready to be listed."

"Just checking. Hoping you might fall in love…with Nantucket, and decide to stay."

Angela smiled. "I do love it here. I will definitely be back to visit, for summer vacations."

"Well, that's good, then."

Angela noticed a car pulling out of the driveway.

"Looks like one of the guests has gone out, so I should probably get started."

~

LATER THAT AFTERNOON, around four, Abby, Kate and Kristen knocked on Angela's front door. She let them in and showed them around as none of them had seen inside her grandmother's cottage since they were children and used to visit.

"They are doing the floors on Monday," she said when she saw Kate looking around the room.

"It's a lovely home. Refinishing the floors will really

make it sparkle. You'll be listing it after that?" Kate asked.

Angela nodded. "Lauren took a bunch of pictures when she was here, but she'll probably want to take a few more to show the hard wood floors."

"It's a tough time of year, but it wouldn't surprise me if you get offers quickly," Abby said. "I was just reading recently that there is still a shortage of real estate inventory all over Massachusetts. It's a great market for a seller."

Angela had mixed feelings about that news. It was bittersweet to think the cottage might sell more quickly than she'd expected. It was great on one hand, but she was really hoping to stay a little longer. Time was going by so fast as it was.

"So, here's all the soap stuff. Let me show you what we need to do." She walked them through the process of heating the oils, stirring the lye and water mixture in and adding the scents before coloring it and pouring it into a mold to cool. They decided to divide the soap into two batches, add some pretty blue and green swirls, and scented one with vanilla and the other with lemongrass.

Once the soap was poured, set aside to cool and everything was cleared up, they ordered pizza. Angela opened a bottle of wine and poured a ginger ale for Abby. They chatted and laughed as they ate the pizza and drank some wine. Kristen was quieter than usual. She'd told them earlier that Tyler was home. She'd met him there for the wake and funeral and he'd stayed on a few days longer to make sure his dad was okay.

They were on their second glasses of wine when Kristen shared a little more about Tyler.

"I'm worried about him. He's taking this really hard. Which is to be expected, but he's withdrawing and shutting me out. I've hardly seen him since he got back. I've called and stopped over to check on him, but he keeps saying he's busy and focusing on his writing."

"Maybe that helps. Losing himself in the writing gives him something to focus on?" Kate suggested.

Kristen nodded. "Maybe, but I feel a little helpless. I just wish I knew what I could do to make him feel better."

"There might not be anything you can do, other than to just be there when he needs you," Abby said. "It might just take time."

Kristen seemed to relax a little as she talked about it. "I think you're probably right. I just hate to see him in so much pain."

"Everyone processes grief different," Kate said.

"You're right. Enough about me, though. I want to hear more about Angela's trip to Boston with Philippe's parents."

Angela had already told them all the highlights. "There's not much more to tell," she said.

"Philippe seems to really like you. He's never had anyone meet his parents before, let alone go on a trip with them. Just wondering if anything has changed between the two of you?"

Angela immediately flashed to the kiss in the Bristol lounge and then pushed the image away and laughed.

"Nothing has changed. We've just become good friends. He's easy to be around."

"Good," Kate said. "I really like both of you and think that's probably for the best, given his track record. If you were going to be staying here, maybe it would be different." She paused for a moment, then laughed and added, "No, it probably wouldn't be. Now that he and Jessica are over, he'll probably be dating someone new any day now."

The thought of it depressed Angela.

"Well, as long as it's not Jessica, I suppose that's fine. He can definitely do better than her," she said.

"I couldn't agree more," Kristen said. "She came into the art gallery when I was doing a show and was rude to one of the salespeople. It was so unnecessary."

"How did it go cleaning her place?" Abby asked.

"Her condo is gorgeous. It's down on the pier and was a gift from her father when she turned twenty-five. Can you imagine?" Angela said.

"So spoiled." Kristen shook her head.

"So what else do we have to do with the soap?" Abby asked.

"It has to sit for twenty-four hours. Then I can cut it, and I'll divide it up for us."

They chatted for another hour or so until Abby began to yawn and everyone decided to head home.

～

NOT LONG AFTER the girls left, Angela realized she'd had a missed message from earlier in the day. It was Beth, Chase's office manager, reminding her that the refinishers were coming first thing Monday morning and that she wouldn't be able to stay in her house for the next four days while they sanded, stained, sealed, and applied the finish coat. She'd totally forgotten about that and Beth had mentioned it when they were first going over the estimate. Shoot, where would she go for the next week?

She hated to impose on anyone. She knew there was no room at the Inn as they were totally booked, plus she had Sam. She supposed she could check with Kristen, but she worried about the damage Sam could cause if he decided to play with one of her paintings. She pulled up her laptop and was searching Airbnb for options that were animal friendly when her cell phone rang. Philippe was calling.

"Hey, there. Did your parents get off okay?"

"They did. I dropped them off at the airport earlier today. We had a great visit. What are you up to?"

"Researching Airbnb's."

"For what?"

"I forgot that Sam and I have to go elsewhere for a

few days while they refinish the floors."

"When are they doing that?"

"First thing Monday."

"Well, that's easy enough. Why don't you come here Sunday night. You and Sam and stay as long as you need to. I have tons of room."

She hadn't even thought of Philippe's place, but he was right, he did have plenty of room.

"Are you sure Mandy won't mind?" She pictured the feisty little cat having an issue with Sam invading her territory.

But Philippe laughed. "Mandy will just have to deal, if she does."

"All right. Thank you. I can't believe I totally forgot about having to leave."

"I'll see you tomorrow night, then. We can get some Thai takeout and watch movies, if that sounds good to you. Have a lazy Sunday."

"Sounds great. What can I bring?"

"Just yourself, and Sam."

∾

PHILIPPE WAS happy to have Angela's company for most of the week. He went out the next day and stocked up on snacks he thought she'd like—popcorn, pub cheese spread and crackers, sliced salami, pepperoni and some crusty, good bread. He also did a load of laundry and put fresh sheets in his best guest bedroom, where his parents had just stayed. It had a king-sized bed and a huge bay window that overlooked the ocean. He remembered that Angela loved looking at the ocean.

She arrived late Sunday afternoon with Sam in his carrier. Mandy came running as usual when she spotted Angela, but she pulled up short when she sensed the presence of another cat. Angela set the carrier down carefully and unzipped the door. Sam tentatively stepped out and stopped when he saw Mandy. It had been a very long time since he'd seen another cat.

Philippe reached down and scratched Sam behind his ears, while Mandy watched with interest. She then took a step towards Sam and sniffed around him while Sam stood frozen, unsure what to do. Finally, Mandy took a final sniff, then spun around and walked off, flicking her tail as she went.

"Well, that didn't go too bad," Philippe said.

Angela laughed. "I wasn't sure what she'd do. As long as Sam gives her plenty of room, I think they'll be okay."

And they were. Every now and then, Mandy took a swipe at Sam, looking to get a rise out of him, but he wouldn't be baited. His usual response was simply to yawn and start giving himself a bath, which greatly disappointed Mandy. After a while, she gave up trying and after a day, Philippe caught her sleeping next to Sam.

Philippe was pleasantly surprised how easy it was to have Angela live with him. They were both pretty easy-going and comfortable with each other. He liked having someone around to talk to, but they also had plenty of comfortable silences where neither one felt like they had to talk. He'd never had that with another girl before. There was usually a sense of pressure to keep a conversation going. With Angela, there was plenty of good conversation as they shared plenty of interests, but sometimes it was nice to just be around another person, enjoying their presence without saying a thing.

They got takeout most nights. Angela left each morning to go to the Inn and returned in the early afternoon. Several of the days she had other cleaning jobs to do, including his. He was somewhat surprised that Jessica had her come again to clean. He'd figured that might be a one-off. She was also going to go to Tyler's again, now that he was back after his mother's funeral.

She was moving back to her place on Friday and Philippe almost hated to see her go. His place was going to feel a bit empty without Angela and Sam.

∽

ANGELA WAS surprised by how easy and fun her week with Philippe had been. She'd thought it might be awkward at times as she was definitely invading his space, but it never felt that way. Even Sam and Mandy were getting along, though every now and then, Mandy liked to remind Sam whose house it was. He was happy to defer to her, though, and his strategy was to just sleep through her moody times.

Tyler had texted a few days ago and asked if she could come by and clean. When she arrived, he answered the door and looked awful, as if he hadn't slept well or shaved in several days. He had dark shadows under his eyes and looked utterly exhausted. He looked glad to see her, though, and smiled slightly.

"Thanks for coming. I'm afraid the place is messier than usual. I have been kind of hibernating since I got home."

"I'm so sorry about your mother. Is your father doing okay?" Angela asked.

He nodded. "Thanks. We're all hanging in as best we can. It was just so unexpected." He held the door open while she came in and set her cleaning supplies and vacuum down.

"I left a check for you on the counter. I'm going to head downtown for a bit. Just lock the door when you leave if you don't mind?"

"Sure thing."

He grabbed his laptop, so Angela guessed he was probably going to the coffee shop to get some writing done. She plugged the vacuum in, turned her music on and started cleaning.

She was just about finished and was dusting in Tyler's bedroom when sunlight coming through the window landed on something sticking out of his open closet. Angela took a closer look and saw that it was a bottle of vodka that was nestled in a pile of dirty clothes in the corner of his closet. She lifted the bottle and saw that it was almost empty except for about an inch of alcohol. Her heart sank as she put it back the way she'd found it and wondered what, if anything she should do with this information.

～

ANGELA WAS DYING to tell someone, so she told Philippe about it later that night while they were snacking on salami, cheese and crackers and sharing a bottle of his good pinot noir.

"Jeez, that's a tough one. If I was Kristen, I'd want to know. But Tyler's your client, so it's an ethical question as to whether to divulge his private information. Especially to his girlfriend. I think I'd lean toward saying nothing."

Angela nodded. "I think so, too. I don't feel right about saying anything as much as I'd like to tell her. I don't think it's my place, or fair to him."

"Maybe there's another way," Philippe began. "What if you subtly just steer her in the right direction, so she can discover it for herself?"

"I'll think about that. And see if the right opportunity presents itself. Maybe he'll just tell her himself, get some help, and go back to meetings?"

"Maybe. Though that might be wishful thinking," Philippe said.

20

L auren had planned to meet Angela at the cottage Friday afternoon. Angela and Sam had moved back in that morning and Angela couldn't get over how beautiful the floors looked now that they'd been refinished. They looked almost brand new and gleamed as the sun shone through the windows and the light fell upon the polished surface. Sam wasn't sure what to think. He walked around sniffing the floors, then running and sliding on them. There was a little bit of a chemical smell still, so Angela opened all the downstairs windows a little to air the house out.

By the time she got home that afternoon, the smell was gone, though the cottage had a slight chill as it was quite cold out. She shut all the windows tight and waited for Lauren to arrive.

She showed up at three o'clock sharp and liked

what she saw. "This really looks fabulous. I'm almost thinking we can start a little higher than I was originally thinking on the price. There is a real shortage of good inventory right now."

"That works for me," Angela said. She followed Lauren around as she took some new pictures, and then had Angela sign the listing agreement that gave Lauren exclusivity for ninety days.

"I don't expect it will take nearly that long. I have a few people already who are waiting to get a look at this."

"Really? You already told some people about it?" Angela was surprised.

Lauren laughed. "Honey, that's what I do. I'm talking to people all the time and everyone wants to be the first to know when something new hits the market. It wouldn't surprise me if this goes fast."

"Oh, okay, then." Angela had it in her mind that it would be at least another month or two before she even had an offer and then another month or two before they closed on the property. Was she ready to leave sooner? She supposed it would be a good problem to have, if the house sold that quickly and for the price that Lauren suggested.

Lauren gathered up the listing sheets, tore a copy off the agreement and handed it to Angela.

"All right, we'll get started then. I'll be in touch when we want to set up showings."

Lauren left and Angela followed right behind her as she was off to clean Jessica's condo.

Jessica was all dressed up and ready to head out the door when Angela arrived. She looked very pretty in a snug, charcoal-colored sweater dress that Angela guessed was likely cashmere.

"Happy New Year!" Jessica said as Angela came in.

"Same to you."

"Did you do anything fun for New Year's Eve?"

Angela hesitated. She sensed that Jessica wouldn't be pleased to know who she was with. So she just said as little as possible.

"I was out of town, actually. What did you do?"

"I had a New Year's Eve party here. Philippe had said he'd try to come, but he didn't show. I'm off to meet him for a drink now, though."

"Oh. Well, have fun."

"Thanks! Your check is on the coffee table. I probably won't be back before you finish."

"I'll make sure to lock the door when I leave."

Angela sighed as Jessica left. She didn't have a good feeling about her meeting with Philippe.

∽

PHILIPPE WAS DREADING his meeting with Jessica. He really didn't want to meet her for a drink, but she insisted and once again it was easy to just agree to appease her.

Plus, he felt a little bad that he'd blown off her New Year's Eve party. Even though they weren't together anymore, he wanted to stay friendly with her. He remained friends with most of the women he dated, except for a few who just didn't take it well when the relationship ended.

They were meeting at the Club Car downtown, one of Philippe's favorite spots to have a cocktail. He arrived on time and Jessica was already there sitting in the most visible spot at the bar, on a corner stool with her long legs crossed. She was wearing a very pretty sweater dress that showed off her curves and her shapely legs. She smiled when she saw him and he gave her a hug and kiss on the cheek before settling onto the stool next to her.

"I hope you weren't waiting long," he said automatically.

"No, not at all. It's great to see you. Did you have a good visit with your family? I'm guessing that's why you didn't make it to my New Year's Eve party."

He nodded as the bartender came over to take their order.

"That's right. We had a great visit. What do you want to drink?"

"Grey Goose and soda for me."

Philippe ordered a draft beer. He wasn't in the mood for anything too strong. The bartender returned a moment later with their drinks.

"So, what did you do with your parents for New Year's Eve?"

"We went to Boston, actually. I was able to get tickets to see the musical Hamilton."

"Oh, that's supposed to be impossible to get tickets for. I'm impressed that you were able to get them."

"You can usually always get tickets. You just might pay a premium for them."

"That's true. Daddy used to do the same thing. That reminds me, if you're interested in joining the country club, he could sponsor you. He's a founding member. We go there often."

"I'm not much of a golfer, unfortunately." He'd never taken to the sport.

"Oh, it's really something you should get better at. So many deals are done on the golf course. All the important people on Nantucket are members."

"Good to know." Philippe glanced at his watch and hoped that Jessica wasn't going to want another drink. How had he not noticed how shallow she was before and how much of a social climber? He supposed that he just hadn't been paying attention. He couldn't help wishing that it was Angela that he was having a drink with instead. He was already missing her energy in the house and Mandy even seemed like she was missing Sam. She'd walked all around the house earlier in the day, looking for him.

"You look like you're millions of miles away," Jessica said.

"Sorry. I'm just tired, I guess."

"So, what else did you do in Boston? Did you go to any good restaurants?"

"We went to the MFA and to dinner at Abe and Louie's."

"I love Abe and Louie's. Did you get the chocolate cake?"

"No, I didn't but my mother and Angela did." As soon as the words were out of his mouth, he regretted it. He'd been thinking about her and spoke without thinking. The air around them suddenly seemed to drop a few degrees.

"Angela went with you? Angela that cleans?"

He nodded. "Yes, she did."

Her eyes narrowed. "Are you dating her now?"

"No, we're just good friends." It was the truth, but Jessica was skeptical.

"Did you ever check a reference on her, before she cleaned for you?" Jessica asked.

"No, of course not. She was referred by a good friend."

"Well, I did. I called the place she last worked for in California and they said that she was fired." Jessica paused dramatically before adding, "For stealing."

Philippe's immediate response was anger for anyone even suggesting that Angela could possibly steal anything.

"I'm sorry, but there must be a mistake. I don't believe that for a minute."

"Well, it's true!"

"So, I assume you're no longer using her, then?" Philippe asked.

Jessica was quiet for a moment. "She's actually cleaning for me right now."

Philippe raised his eyebrows, finished his drink and reached in his wallet to pay the tab.

Jessica pouted. "I thought we'd have another."

"I have to get going." He didn't have to be anywhere, but he had no interest in staying with Jessica a moment longer than he needed to.

She took the last sip of her drink and then tried one last time. "There's an event at the club next weekend, a wine dinner for a good cause. I don't remember what it is, but everyone important in town will be there. We should go. I have an extra ticket."

"I may be going skiing next weekend. Have fun, Jessica." It wasn't a complete lie. He had thought about going skiing again soon. Though it probably wasn't going to be quite that soon.

"Oh, okay. I guess I'll see you around, then."

Philippe walked her to her car and said goodbye. He was looking forward to a quiet night at home with Mandy.

∽

ANGELA WAS JUST FINISHING up when Jessica came storming into the condo. She glared at Angela when she saw her.

"I can't believe you went to Boston with Philippe!"

Angela said nothing. Philippe had obviously told her.

"I called that place you used to work. You know, Happy Cleaners. And I told Philippe why you were fired. I don't think I'll be needing you to clean for me again."

Angela coolly picked up her check and tucked it in her pocket. She was fine with not working for Jessica again.

"I know that you called Nora. She told me when she called to offer me my job back. She also told me that she told you that I never stole anything. I don't suppose you told Philippe that part of the story, did you? I'm sure Philippe also told you that we're just friends."

"Just go!" Jessica stomped off toward her bedroom and Angela gladly left.

#

When she got home, she called Philippe and he answered on the first ring.

"I thought I might hear from you. Did you run into Jessica?"

"I did. She told me that she told you why I was fired, but I don't think she told you the part where they apologized, called and offered me my job back and said the daughter of the woman who demanded I be fired actually confessed to stealing her mother's bracelet."

Philippe chuckled. "No, she left that part out. I

knew you didn't steal anything, though. I don't think she believes that we are just friends."

"Too bad."

"That's right. Too bad. It doesn't matter what she thinks. So, did you get your house listed?"

"I did. It's officially on the market now. Lauren seems to think it might go quickly."

Philippe was quiet for a moment. "Selfishly, I hope it doesn't. But if that's what you want, then I wish you a speedy sale."

Angela smiled. "Thank you. You're a good friend."

"Best ever. I'll call you soon. Let's go see a movie or grab some dinner."

"I'd like that."

21

L auren called as Angela was ending the call with Philippe.

"I have three people that want to come see your house tomorrow. Are you flexible on time?" she asked.

Angela didn't expect that she would show the house so quickly.

"Sure, anytime works. I'll be gone until two but can stay away longer."

"Okay, I'll get back to you with specific times. Thanks." Lauren ended the call and texted her soon after with the confirmed times that she'd be bringing people by. Angela found herself suddenly feeling anxious but then told herself that was silly. Just because a few people were coming to look at the house, didn't mean that there would be any offers.

∾

LAUREN CALLED Angela Sunday afternoon and her excitement was evident.

"We have a bidding war! Two of the people that looked at your cottage fell in love with it. I told them it's a multiple bid situation and they need to make their best offer. I'll be back to you later today with more details. Just wanted to let you know the good news.

"Thanks. That's great news."

Angela hung up the phone and didn't feel nearly as excited as she'd imagined she would when she got the news that an offer was coming. Depending on the terms of the offer, her time on Nantucket could be coming to an end much sooner than expected.

She scooped up Sam and snuggled with him on the sofa, watching Hallmark movies for the rest of the afternoon. She was on pins and needles waiting for Lauren's call to come. It was crazy to her to think that someone might spend upwards of two million dollars for her grandmother's cottage. It was so much money, and she reminded herself that it was what she wanted, to go home to San Francisco with money in the bank. Jane would be thrilled, and it would be nice to see her best friend again.

But she'd made so many new friends on Nantucket. It was going to be hard to leave them all behind. She would have money, though, to come back for visits. She felt like she was on vacation everyday and hated to think of her time on the island drawing to a close. She imagined that was how the summer residents felt, when September rolled around and it was time to close their cottages and head back to wherever home was.

The call came a little after six.

"Do you have a pen? I can email both offers over but wanted to give you the quick details. They're both very good offers."

"Okay, I'm ready." As ready as she'd ever be.

"So, the offers are close, but I think one is stronger than the other. Both are just over two million, but one offer is all cash and they'd like to close as soon as possible. You could have your money in thirty days. What do you think?"

"Thirty days? Wow."

"I know, right? I'll email them over now and why don't you take the night and call me in the morning?"

"I'll do that."

Lauren's email came a few minutes later and Angela looked them over carefully. One offer was cash. The other was contingent on selling another property. That meant it was less of a sure thing and could drag the process out. As much as Angela hated for her time on the island to end, she also hated uncertainty even more. The cash offer was more solid and they could schedule the closing date as soon as possible. In a month, she could have a huge check in hand and be on her way back to San Francisco. It was bittersweet but it was what she'd planned to do, what made the most sense for her future.

She called Lauren in the morning and accepted the cash offer.

"Congratulations! I'll drop by this afternoon to have you sign the offer."

"Thank you."

$\sim$

LISA WAS happy for her when she shared the news at breakfast but said that she would miss her.

"I really hate to see you go. It's a lot of money, though. I imagine that would be hard to turn down. You can have a fresh start now."

"I'll still be here for another month. Will you be able to find someone after that?" Angela worried about Lisa trying to do too much and hurting her back.

"You're sweet to worry. I'll be able to manage. It's just a few weeks after that and Harriet will be back. She sent me a Christmas card reminding me of the date. Plus, I've been doing yoga almost every day and I think my back is getting stronger."

"I'll miss all of you." Angela was already dreading saying goodbye.

"We'll all miss you, too. I know I will, and the girls and I'm sure Philippe, too."

Angela smiled. "I'll come back for vacations whenever I can."

"Of course you will. Though you'll be busy with that new job you'll be getting."

"That won't be for a while yet. I still have two classes to finish up first. I'll probably see if I can take them during the summer session. Classes are already starting soon for the spring."

"Well, whatever you do, I know you'll be a success. And whenever you're ready to come for a visit, we'll be here."

∼

JANE WAS over the moon when Angela called her with the news.

"Yay! You should come back for a visit before you move home, so you can look at a few rentals and line something up to move right into. You're always welcome, of course, to stay here."

Angela preferred to get her own place and not subject Jane and her allergies to Sam.

"Maybe I'll fly out for a long weekend and see if I can line up a few places to look at." It was all moving so fast, but it made sense to be smart about it.

She called Kate and Kristen next to give them the news and to also see if either of them would mind covering for her if she flew home for the weekend. They both said they'd be happy to help.

"Of course we will," Kate said. "I'm happy to do it, and I'm sure Kristen will be, too. Maybe she'll do one of the days and I'll do the others. We'll figure it out. We will miss you, though."

She called Abby next and she echoed what her sisters had said. Her last call was to Philippe and he congratulated her but was quieter than usual.

"I wish you weren't going," he admitted. "But I am happy for you."

∼

THE NEXT TWO weeks flew by as Angela tried to spend as much time with everyone as possible and also got ready to move home. She bought her tickets and dropped Sam off with Philippe, who volunteered to watch him while she was gone.

The day she was due to fly to San Francisco, a thick letter came from her grandmother's law firm in Boston. It was a handwritten note from Warren and a typed letter from her grandmother. She read Warren's note first.

Dear Angela,

I hope you are doing well. I had instructions from your grandmother to mail this letter to you a month after you arrived on Nantucket. She wanted you to have some time to settle in and appreciate the island first.

Wishing you a Happy New Year,
Warren

ANGELA UNFOLDED the letter from her grandmother. She recognized the paper and look of the type as likely coming from her old Olympia typewriter.

My dearest girl,

I don't have much time, they say. Maybe just a few days at this point, I'm not really sure. I have my good days and my bad, but know it won't be long. I'm home and I'm comfortable. The hospice nurses are truly wonderful people. But enough about me. I wanted to tell you a bit about your history and why we never met before now.

Your mother was my only child and was a handful. She was kind-hearted, but impulsive and easily influenced. It was her big heart that got her into trouble when she fell in with the wrong crowd in high school. She tried things that she shouldn't have, even though she knew better. But, I know now that she couldn't help herself. She suffered from addiction, as I suspect you well know.

We had some hard times with Chrissy. I tried my best to help her, but nothing seemed to work and the only thing left was to turn her away. It was the hardest thing I've ever done, what I was advised to do and I did it to help her find her way. I don't know if it was the right decision or not. I've struggled with that all my life, because I lost my daughter because of it. She never forgave me, and she never came back. And I never knew you even existed until today. My biggest regret is that I never got to know you. I hope I can make that up to you somewhat by leaving you my cottage on Nantucket, the happiest place I know. I hope that it brings you joy and I wish you a long and very happy life.

With all my love, your grandmother,
Estelle Stark.

ANGELA COULD HARDLY SEE through the tears that were freely falling. It hurt that she'd never known her grand-mother and she ached for her loss, for hoping she'd done the right thing, and not getting the outcome that she'd hoped. Angela wished that she could tell her that it wasn't her fault. That Chrissy was just broken, damaged beyond help by an addiction that she couldn't beat.

She looked around the cottage and a fresh wave of tears came. She'd felt such peace here. It was going to be sad to leave the cottage and all of its history behind.

∼

ANGELA TOOK an Uber to the Nantucket airport, flew to Boston and then on to San Francisco. Jane picked her up at the airport. She was thrilled to see her and went with her to look at the apartments that Angela had found online.

They were all fine, lovely even, and Angela would

have been happy in any of them. It was difficult to choose, and truth be told, she wasn't ready to give a deposit and make the commitment just yet. The realtor that showed them around was understanding, though.

"Here's my card. Just give me a call when you make up your mind and we can take a deposit check over the phone."

Angela had the money in her account, since there was enough money to cover several months of expenses. She'd been mostly using the money she made from her cleaning work, so she could write a check anytime.

"Which one did you like best?" Jane asked as they drove back to her house.

"I don't really know. They were all fine, all good locations."

"That's true. You really can't go wrong with any of them. I'm so glad you're moving back sooner than expected. And I'm so happy for you."

Angela smiled. "Thanks. It doesn't seem real, to be honest."

"It will when you get that check in your hands."

22

I t looks like Jessica has moved on," Kate said. They were all at the Irish Pub on the Friday night after Angela went to San Francisco.

Philippe smiled when he saw who Jessica was with. Sean Prescott was a well-known developer. He was visible in town and a member of the country club Jessica was so enamored with. In short, he was perfect for her. And Philippe hoped that it would work out. Jessica turned a corner and just like that, she was gone from Philippe's thoughts, too.

It was Angela who was on his mind. She wasn't there yet and Philippe looked every time the front door opened, to see if it was her. He hadn't seen her since she'd stopped by his house on her way home from San Francisco, to pick up Sam.

He'd been surprised by how much he'd missed her. Just knowing she was across the country all weekend had depressed him. Ever since she'd stayed with him for almost a week while her floors were being done, something had shifted inside him. He'd never missed someone like this when they weren't around. He'd always been more than happy to go out and have a wonderful time with someone, then go home and sleep alone or if they spent the night or the weekend, he was always relieved when they went home and he had his place to himself again.

It wasn't like that with Angela. Ever since she'd stayed with him, his house felt empty without her there. It really scared him when she went away for the long weekend because it was a wakeup call that if he didn't do something soon, she'd be gone for good. And it was becoming more and more apparent to him that he didn't want her to go. He needed her to stay.

But, he didn't know if she shared his feelings. They'd had that one, wonderful kiss in Boston on New Year's Eve, but they'd both pulled back after that. Angela was hard to read. He knew that she liked his company and he sensed that maybe she was attracted to him, too, if their kiss was anything to go by. But he also knew that she was resisting it.

And he couldn't blame her. He didn't exactly have the best track record. But he knew in his soul that things were different now. That he was different, when he was with her. And that he needed to tell her how he felt, before it was too late.

The door opened again, and this time it was

Angela. She smiled and waved when she saw Philippe and the others and made her way over to them. There was a big group out for the night—Kate and Jack, Chase and Beth, and Kristen and Tyler. Philippe thought about what Angela had said about Tyler and noticed that he seemed tense and fidgety and kept looking at the bar. But Tyler was drinking a soda, so that was good at least. Philippe hoped that Tyler was back on the wagon. He sympathized, guessing that it must be difficult to be out around other people who were drinking when you were trying not to.

Angela ordered a chardonnay and sat on the empty stool next to Philippe.

Beth and Chase were sitting on the other side of her.

"We already had a call from the people that made an offer on your house," Beth said.

"Oh, really? They want to make some changes?"

Beth and Chase exchanged glances and Chase laughed.

"To put it mildly. They want to do a major renovation. A total upgrade, putting in all marble counters in the kitchen and bathroom, stainless steel appliances, AGA stove. They want to rip up your newly refinished hardwood floors and put in heated ones everywhere. She's from Florida, I guess. And they asked about putting in a Cathedral ceiling."

"Is that even possible?" Angela asked.

"Anything is possible. But that would be a major

renovation. I recommended against it. It doesn't fit the character of the place, but it's not my house."

Angela tried to picture her grandmother's house with the changes that Chase had mentioned and it was a depressing image. It just seemed wrong to modernize it that much. It would lose all of its rustic charm. And the polished hard wood floors looked so pretty. The idea of it made her all the more sad about leaving Nantucket and giving up her grandmother's house.

A little while later, Kristen stopped over to chat. Tyler was nowhere to be seen.

"He went home. Said he wasn't feeling well. He's been under a lot of pressure lately and has a deadline looming."

"How is he doing with the loss of his mother?" Angela asked.

"He doesn't talk about it much. But I can tell that it's still really hard for him. He's cancelled plans with me twice lately, saying that he just isn't up for going out. I'm worried about him. I think maybe he might be dealing with some depression of some sort, and needs to talk to someone that can help him get through this."

"That might be a good idea," Philippe agreed.

Angela glanced his way and their eyes met. He knew she was still concerned with what she'd seen in Tyler's closet. He felt she'd made the right decision to respect his privacy, though. That kind of grief was difficult and Tyler need to find his way somehow.

By the end of the night, it was just Angela and

Philippe left at the bar. Everyone else had gone home, but they were still deep in conversation. Angela had switched to a hot coffee drink and Philippe had been sipping a snifter of Grand Marnier for over an hour, savoring the sweet orange taste and wanting to make the evening last longer. He was trying to get his courage up to really talk to Angela.

"I can't believe those buyers want to change my grandmother's house so much," Angela said again. He could tell that the news bothered her as she'd said the same thing earlier.

"I wouldn't do it. But once people buy something, they can do whatever they want with it."

Angela sighed. "I know. But it just seems wrong."

He smiled. "I agree." He looked around the bar and no one was in ear shot. "Now that we're alone, there's something that I want to say to you."

"Oh? What's that?" She looked curious, but he could tell she had no idea what was coming next.

"I really don't want you to go. I want to be more than friends with you, Angela. Much more. I started to realize it when you and Sam stayed with me. The house just wasn't the same when you guys left. I think even Mandy missed you both."

Angela's eyes grew wide and she sucked in her breath. He'd surprised her.

"When you went to Boston with my parents it was just so easy. It's always easy being with you and fun. They loved you by the way."

She smiled. "I loved them, too."

"Here's the thing. I'm not sure how you feel about me, but I just had to let you know how I feel before you moved back to San Francisco. I think I'm falling in love with you. This is new for me, and a little scary," he confessed.

Angela was dead silent and looked completely shocked. And he wasn't sure if that was a good thing.

"Say something. Either put me out of my misery or make me the happiest man alive and tell me that maybe you might possibly feel even remotely the same way."

~

ANGELA'S HEART was pounding like crazy and she felt light-headed. She also felt a sense of joy so strong that she couldn't help but grin.

"I do. I feel the same way. I tried not to. You don't have the best track record, you know."

He took her hand and squeezed it. "I know. I'm sorry about that."

She laughed. "Are you serious? Really and truly serious?"

"More than I've ever been. I meant it when I said the house feels empty without you. I don't care if you sell your house or not, but don't move to San Francisco. Move in with me instead."

"You want me to move in with you?"

"I do. We can get engaged if you want. I have a ring. I just didn't want to completely overwhelm you and have you think I'm a crazy person."

"I don't think you're crazy. And I do think I want to move in with you, but not right away. Let's officially date for at least a month or two first. I'll cancel the house sale."

"Great, whatever you want to do is fine. Did you put a deposit down on an apartment?"

"No, I couldn't do it. I put it off. I really don't want to leave Nantucket. I don't want to leave you."

"Then don't. Stay here, with me. Forever."

"Okay."

"Let's go home—to your future home, that is." Philippe pulled her toward him and kissed her with everything that he felt. When the kiss ended, Angela's head was spinning but in a good way. Finally, she felt like with Philippe, she was really and truly home.

EPILOGUE

Two months later

S he's getting so big," Angela said.

"I know, isn't she beautiful? I'm madly in love with her. I suppose all grandmothers feel that way?"

They were having breakfast at the Inn and Lisa was babysitting while Abby and Jeff spent a weekend away.

"She is beautiful," Angela agreed. "I miss this, our morning breakfasts." Lisa had invited her to stop by and catch up as it had been over a month since she'd finished up cleaning the rooms, since Harriet came back.

"Well, you can stop by anytime, you know that. Although, you're probably too busy now with all the new cleaning business you've been booking."

Angela laughed. "It is going pretty well, I have to

admit. I never imagined I'd be starting my own company instead of working for someone else."

"All those marketing and business classes were put to good use. And you're doing your last two online? So you'll have your bachelor degree soon?"

"I will. It's been a long time coming, but I wanted to make sure I finished and earned the degree."

Angela smiled. "It's funny the twists and turns that life takes. It never occurred to me before to try and make a business out of cleaning."

"Do what you love and the money will follow. I heard that years ago. It seems to be true from what I've seen," Lisa said.

Angela nodded. There definitely was some truth to the old saying. She had been surprised by how quickly word spread when she let people know she was looking to grow her cleaning business. She even got a referral from Jessica, even though she wasn't cleaning for her anymore! She guessed that there was a little bit of guilt involved in that. She'd also heard that Jessica just got engaged to Sean Prescott, the prominent business man, so she was probably over the moon with that accomplishment.

Angela wasn't engaged herself yet, though Philippe had told her that he had the ring ready and all she had to do was say the word. For now, she was very happy living with him, and simply enjoying each day as it happened. She'd moved in a month ago and as she'd suspected, it was an easy transition. Their two cats got along well enough too, except for the occasional moment when Mandy was in a mood—they even took the occasional nap together.

And she was thrilled that Jane booked a week in July to stay at Angela's cottage. Jane had wanted to pay the going rate, but Angela wouldn't hear of it. She'd decided to keep her grandmother's house and rent it out. She couldn't bear the thought of the house being changed so drastically and she wasn't ready to let go of it.

She also liked having a place of her own to call home if she needed to, and she really liked the monthly rental income, which supplemented her cleaning work. Jane had been disappointed at first when Angela told her she was going to be staying on Nantucket. She hadn't been surprised though.

"I'll miss you, but I always had a feeling by the way you talked about Philippe and Nantucket that you weren't going to be coming home."

∼

LATER THAT EVENING, when she and Philippe were relaxing in the living room, after eating bowls of pasta and meatballs and watching the evening news, Philippe took her hand and smiled.

"I just want you to know, I love having you and Sam living here. I can't imagine my life without you in it. I love you Angela Stark."

Angela sighed, feeling full and happy. "I love you too, Philippe. I didn't expect this, wasn't looking for it, but I'm so glad that I found it, with you."

∾

THANK you so much for reading! I hope you enjoyed this book, and I'd be very grateful if you took the time to leave a quick review. It helps new readers find the books. =)

Next up in the series is A NANTUCKET AFFAIR, which has a bit of a double meaning when one of Lisa's best friends, Sue, has a husband who is coordinating a yearly charity affair on the beach—with the help of their younger, gorgeous, and very blonde new employee, Brandi. Find out more, here.

In the meantime, have you read TRUST, the very first book I wrote? If you like women's fiction with a bit of suspense, you might enjoy it.

EXCERPT OF TRUST

Three weeks before the wedding, your fiancé becomes a person of interest in a murder investigation. What would you do?

In TRUST, 36-year-old, high school teacher Lauren seems to have it all. She moved back to Waverly, a small seaside town, just north of Boston, MA several years ago. She has a great career, and has finally found true love. Lauren's wedding is just a few weeks away, when one of her students goes missing and when his body is found a few days later, she suddenly becomes a person of interest.

Her fiancé, Tyler, is a former minor-league pitcher turned stockbroker, who is excited to settle down with Lauren. But when the missing student is found dead, and the media turns its attention even more closely on

Lauren, Tyler is surprised to discover that Lauren hadn't told him everything about her past.

With the help of his 91-year-old grandfather, who is a retired town sheriff, and his best friend Jake, the current assistant sheriff, Tyler sets out to find the truth.

Prologue

Twenty years earlier....

Melissa Hopkins wanted more than anything to be home in her warm bed, securely tucked under her thick down comforter. For several hours now, she'd been sitting in a small windowless room at the local police headquarters, being interrogated by the same two cops non-stop. It made her head ache, although she supposed the drinks she'd had earlier could be a contributor to that as well.

Most of her friends had started drinking a few years ago, around age fourteen. It was common in Waverly, a beachfront community that was busy in the summer and deadly deserted in the winter months. Her friends considered her a lightweight, as she had always said no, until a few months ago on her sixteenth birthday.

Melissa closed her eyes and tried to focus, and to remember what really happened, but her memory was a confused blur. She suspected she might have blacked out for a bit. That had happened once before when she'd been drinking vodka, and this time they had been playing quarters on the beach and doing shots. It was hard to play well on the sand, plus someone had the bright idea to mix vodka with orange juice and made the losers slug shots of the drink instead of beer. Melissa's stomach did an unhappy flip just thinking about it.

"Melissa, your Mom is waiting outside to take you home. As soon as you tell us what we need to hear, you'll be on your way. You want to go home Melissa, don't you?" The police officers seemed to taunt her. One was a tough looking Irish guy in his mid-thirties, who was clearly frustrated. The other cop was younger looking and equally irritated. They started in again, asking the questions they'd already asked, but this time she was hearing them differently. Her mind was too tired to protest.

"Melissa, the other two boys saw you run after Nancy with the murder weapon. Your prints are all over it, along with her blood. You were mad at Nancy —you admitted that already. You obviously did this, Melissa."

Melissa's head started to throb and she pressed a hand against her forehead, willing the pain to go away. "They saw me run after Nancy? Holding something?" It was so hard to focus. She had been mad at Nancy, furious even, but still, she wouldn't have killed her. She was sure of it. But it was all a bit hazy. She remembered running, falling and then waking up to a police officer shaking her and a flashlight in her face. She was still very confused and scared and was just sober enough to know that she was in serious trouble. Was there a chance that she could have done this? The police seemed to think so, and they said they had proof.

"Yes, Melissa. Just admit you killed her; all the evidence makes it very clear. If you confess, things will go much easier for you. You could be looking at much less jail time; a huge difference Melissa. We don't think you meant to do this. You didn't mean to kill her, right Melissa?"

"No, I didn't mean to kill her." Melissa felt bewildered, like she was being pulled underwater or in some kind of surreal dream.

"Say you killed her and you can go home. We can all go home." Their voices were kinder and softer now and Melissa really, really wanted to go home. She'd lost track of how many hours she'd been in this room, but it was much too long.

"I guess maybe I did it, I'm not really sure. I must have though, right?"

"Yes, good girl, Melissa. We'll go get your mother."

∾

Chapter 1

Lauren Stanhope stared out the window at the falling snow and marveled at the picture-perfect scene outside. It was just starting to get dark, and the dusky pink sky cast a warm glow over the neighborhood, which was a collection of meticulously maintained Victorian homes, many with intricate gingerbread woodwork now delicately frosted in a light covering of snow.

"You girls are so tiny," Nellie Chapman said as she pulled in the fabric around Lauren's waist tight and jabbed in a pin to mark the spot.

Lauren's friend and soon to be sister-in-law, Amy, snickered at that and Lauren shot her a look. Nellie was a sweetheart, and a close friend of the family, but she was also in her early 80's, and though she did fabulous work as a seamstress, she'd made the same comment at the bridesmaid fitting for Amy's wedding and took all their dresses in so much that they popped loose whenever they moved the wrong way. Though she'd agreed to use Nellie, Lauren wasn't going to let that happen again.

"Could you please leave it a little looser than you normally would? I have a tendency to gain weight when I'm stressed out. Better safe than sorry right?"

Nellie pushed her glasses back in place and glared at the spot she'd just pinned. With a painful sigh, she whipped out the pin and let some material out.

"I don't like it," she muttered as she jabbed the pin back in to its new spot.

"Thank you, that's perfect." Lauren smiled at the older woman who was still frowning at the beautiful wedding dress.

"Okay dear, leave it here in the dressing room. Amy and I will wait for you in the den."

Once Nellie and Amy left, Lauren peeled off the wedding dress and climbed back into her work clothes of gray flannel trousers and a soft caramel cashmere sweater. She peeked out the tiny window in the dressing room and got another little thrill from the sight of the falling snow. The first snowfall of the year always affected her that way; she got as excited as a little kid at the sight of the fat snowflakes drifting down. The cozy scene made her think of the warm feeling she always felt around the holidays and how she'd longed for years to create her own family and try to capture and keep that magical feeling all year.

Lauren still couldn't believe how much her life had changed in the past two years, moving back here, meeting Tyler, falling in love and actually having that love returned. She was tempted to pinch herself because it really did seem too good to be true that in a little over a month she'd be married and on her way to having the perfect life that she'd always dreamed of. She would hopefully even have a new home since she and Tyler had been house hunting and found several houses that had potential. Still, she couldn't shake the feeling that it could all slip away in a moment, and that she was crazy to think she deserved to have that kind of happiness. She knew how quickly things could change when you least expected it. But, she reminded herself that it was just the nerves talking, and that it was normal for a bride-to-be to experience pre-wedding jitters.

"Lauren, your student is on TV, come quick," Amy called. She was one of the first people Lauren had met when she moved to town, as they were both teachers at the local high school. Lauren crossed the hall into a small sitting room, where Amy and Nellie were sitting on a cozy sofa and watching the news on a big screen TV.

"His name is Eric, right?" Amy asked, as the photo of the young teen flashed across the screen.

"Yes, Eric Armstrong. He's been out for the past three days. I thought he was sick. The flu has been going around something fierce."

"It's not the flu. He's missing. Do you think he might have run away?"

Lauren thought for a moment. "It's possible. I know he's been having some issues at home. We've met a few times after school recently, trying to figure out a way to help him focus better in class."

"Poor kid," Amy said.

"Let's hope he just ran away," Nellie said, voicing what they'd all been thinking. At least if he ran away there was a good chance he'd come back.

Chapter 2

Tyler Bishop had a standing dinner date every Tuesday night at Hannigan's Pub. His grandfather was already seated at his usual booth when Tyler arrived and joined him.

"Glad you could make it," was his grandfather's usual greeting, as if there was any doubt that Tyler would be there. Both of them looked forward to these dinners. At ninety-one years of age, Gramps was all Tyler had left for family and he really did enjoy his company. Gramps was still as sharp as a tack and had more energy than many people half his age. It had been difficult for Tyler when he lost his mother to lung cancer just over two years ago, and his grandfather had been through a lot too, as he had also lost his wife. Tyler's grandmother had passed away around that same time. Tyler never failed to be inspired by him. Instead of shutting down, his grandfather had blossomed and turned into a social butterfly. Though the food was good at Hannigan's, his grandfather freely admitted that the people—particularly the young friendly waitresses who showered him with attention and laughed at his jokes—were the reason he came as often as he did.

"Tyler, do you know Allison?" Gramps was chatting with a pretty blonde waitress who had just delivered his drink, a frothy Kahlua sombrero. Gramps wasn't a big drinker, but often had a single sombrero, which he said reminded him of a milkshake.

"Hi, Allison," Tyler said as he sat down across from his grandfather.

"Tyler's my grandson. He's getting married in a

month." His grandfather beamed at that. He was a huge fan of Lauren.

Tyler ordered a beer and they decided to split a pizza. They both agreed that the best thing on Hannigan's menu was the bar pizza. The rumor was that they'd bought the recipe from a restaurant in the next county. The crust was unusual, crisp and a little flaky. The tomato sauce was fresh and sweet and there was always plenty of cheese. Best of all, on Tuesday nights they ran a buy-one get-one special.

"This is the best deal in town," Gramps announced with enthusiasm as Allison set two steaming pizzas in front of them. As he always did, Tyler agreed with him, and they dug in.

"Pity about that missing kid. It's been on the news all afternoon. You hear anything from Jake about it?" His grandfather asked as he reached for his third slice.

"No. I haven't talked to him in a few days. He's meeting me here a little later though for a drink. Have your guys heard anything?" Gramps had served as the town sheriff for many years and still kept in touch with some of the current officers who were sons of his former men. There was a small group of officers, most retired for many years, who met up every Saturday for lunch. Gramps probably knew almost as much as Jake did about what was going on in town, and Jake was the current assistant sheriff.

"Just sounds like he ran away. Shame, that. Kids feeling like they have to run away." Gramps finished off the last bite of pizza on his plate and dabbed at the side of his mouth with a napkin. "That was damn good, as usual."

"You should stay and have a drink with Jake. He should be here soon. He'd love to see you." Tyler reached for the last slice; as usual, they'd easily finished one pizza and Gramps would take the leftovers home.

Gramps considered that for a moment. "Tell him I said hello. I can't stay though. I've had my one drink for the night; if I have another I'll be plastered."

Tyler smiled at that. They both knew Gramps had never been 'plastered' a day in his life. One drink was all he ever wanted.

"Besides, Dancing with the Stars is on tonight. You know I never miss that. It's the results show." He was serious about that. Gramps was an excellent dancer and it was something he and his grandmother had always enjoyed, as she was a professional dancer when they first met.

After they paid the bill and his grandfather left, Tyler moved to the bar to wait for Jake. The bar was getting packed now and he'd only just settled into his seat and taken his first sip of a newly poured beer, when someone bumped into the back of his chair, hard enough that he spilled a good half-inch of his beer.

In a second, Patrick, the bartender was there to mop up the mess. "Give me your mug," he demanded and Tyler handed it over, watching with appreciation as Patrick topped it off and set it back down again.

"There you are then, good as new." That was another reason they liked coming here. Hannigan's was a real Irish pub, the type of place where everyone really did know your name and if they didn't, it wouldn't be long before they did. They made you feel like a regular no matter how often you visited.

"Hey man, sorry about that," said a deep voice to his left. As it turned out, the man who'd spilled his beer was Randy Scribbs, a former fraternity brother that Tyler hadn't seen in nearly fifteen years. Randy looked about the same. He was still a huge guy, well over 6' 2" and had dark curly hair that had thinned quite a bit over the years, not that Tyler could say much there. He had grown to like the baseball cap look more and more for the same reason.

"Randy, what brings you to town? It's been a long time."

"My wife, Sharon, is pregnant and her family lives nearby, so we decided to buy a place here. I travel a lot for work and this way she'll have support close by."

"That's great," Tyler said, glancing around the bar. Jake was running late as usual. He'd called earlier, said he had something important to tell him, and wanted to meet for an after work drink.

"So, I hear you got out of the baseball business?" Randy's cheerful voice boomed above the crowd, and if you didn't know better, you'd think he was just a friendly guy. As if Tyler had chosen to 'get out of the baseball business.' He'd been a rising star once, the scouts had all buzzed about his 'nasty stuff', the ultimate honor bestowed on pitching prospects. Until he blew out his arm in his third major-league start with the Boston Red Sox. A freak accident they called it and immediately shipped him off for the usual cure, Tommy-John surgery. But his arm was never the same and his career in baseball came to a quick end.

"Yeah, I got sick of it, too much travel." Tyler took a long sip of beer and wished for a quick end to this reunion.

"Very funny. You were always a funny guy." Randy looked at him thoughtfully before adding, "I heard you're pretty good with numbers. Mark Tsongas said I should look you up."

Tyler didn't see this coming at all. Mark was his biggest client and he wouldn't have guessed that he knew Randy.

"Yeah, I manage Mark's investment portfolio. We did okay last year."

"I heard it was way better than okay," Randy said with an enthusiasm that made Tyler cringe. Where the hell was Jake? He glanced at his watch as Randy continued, "Mark golfs with Sharon's brother. I played with them last week and asked if they knew of a good broker. I sold one of my companies a few months ago and have a little money I need to invest. Do you have a card?"

"Sure, here you go." Tyler dug into his wallet and then handed him a business card. When he looked up, he saw that Jake had finally arrived and was looking around the packed bar. Tyler waved him over and Jake squeezed into the seat next to him as Randy turned to leave.

"Gotta run. I'll call your office to set up a meeting. Great seeing you. Oh, hey, Mark also mentioned you're getting married in a few weeks. Hope this one works out better for you!" Randy slapped him on the back in farewell and then he was gone.

"Who was that asshole?" Jake asked as Patrick set his usual beer down in front of him.

"You really don't want to know. He's a former fraternity brother who just moved to town. The good news is, I probably have a new client. Bad news is, I have to deal with him."

Randy would have to remind him of Jillian. Even though it was over ten years ago, it still hurt to think of how she'd dumped him barely two weeks before their wedding because she 'just didn't love him enough.' You don't just bounce right back from something like that. He'd pretty much given up on the whole love and family thing until he met Lauren when she moved to town two years ago.

He'd always been skeptical of love at first sight, but he definitely felt it when his sister Amy, a ninth grade teacher, introduced him to her new colleague, Lauren. Lauren had lived in the area years ago into her early teens, and said she'd applied 'on a whim' when she'd seen the advertised opening. It was very different with

Lauren. He knew she'd never pull the rug out from under him the way Jillian had. It was just easy with her because they got along great and trusted each other completely.

"Tyler? Did you hear me?" Jake was looking at him expectantly. And he hadn't heard a word he'd said.

"Oh, sorry. I was just distracted for a minute. What did you say?"

"So you know that missing student? Eric Armstrong?"

"Yeah, I think he was one of Lauren's kids. Any word on him yet?" If there were any news, Jake would likely know of it.

"Nothing yet. The parents swear he'd never run away. That doesn't mean much though. Kids run away all the time." He paused for a minute, then added, "Did Lauren ever mention him at all? Say anything about him?"

"Are you asking as a friend or a police officer?" Tyler teased. But the serious look on Jake's face told him he didn't think it was funny.

"Both, I guess. We're just digging everywhere we can, hoping to turn up something."

"Sorry. You know Lauren did mention that she'd been talking to him, trying to help him work through some things."

"What kind of things?"

"His grades had been slipping and it wasn't great at

home. That's all I know. I'm not sure if Lauren knows much more than that."

"She didn't say anything else? Nothing else about the boy at all?"

"No, why? Has something turned up about him?"

"Nothing definitive. We've been going through his computer records and his online diary."

"Online diary? As in available to the public?"

"Yeah, connected to his Facebook page. Kids these days live their lives online—totally bizarre."

"Does he say anything that might give a clue as to if or why he ran away?"

"No. But he does talk about having a 'mad crush' on a much older woman. Someone he thinks about and sees every day."

Tyler felt a sudden sinking in his stomach. "Do you have any idea who this 'older woman' is?"

"Nothing concrete, but we have to consider all possibilities and the strongest one we have so far is that it very well could be Lauren."

∾

Made in the USA
Middletown, DE
27 February 2021